Mary Sullivan

Stay

A NOVEL

ZOLAND BOOKS
Cambridge, Massachusetts

First edition published in 2000 by
Zoland Books, Inc.
384 Huron Avenue
Cambridge, Massachusettes 02138

PUBLISHER'S NOTE

This book is a work of fiction. Names, characters, places, and
incidents are either the product of the author's imagination or are
used fictitiously. Any resemblance to actual events or persons,
living or dead, is entirely coincidental.

FIRST EDITION

Book design by Boskydell Studio
Printed in the United States of America

06 05 04 03 02 01 00   8 7 6 5 4 3 2 1

This book is printed on acid-free paper, and its binding materials
have been chosen for strength and durability.

Library of Congress Cataloging-in-Publication-Data

Sullivan, Mary, 1966–
Stay : a novel / Mary Sullivan. — 1st ed.
p.   cm.
ISBN 1-58195-025-X (acid-free paper)
1. Brothers — Death — Fiction.   2. Mute persons — Fiction.
3. Twins — Fiction.   4. Girls — Fiction.   I. Title.

PS3569.U3483 S7 2000
813'.6 — dc21
00-033442
CIP

For Christopher Colbourn

Thank you to my family
for their love and support,
and also to Sara Brock
and my agent Lane Zachary.

We were as twinn'd lambs that did frisk i' th' sun,
And bleat the one at th' other. What we chang'd
Was innocence for innocence.

William Shakespeare
The Winter's Tale

Stay

1

"Time for confession," my sister whispers in my ear. "You better talk to us or you'll end up like you know who."

I follow Hope through the kitchen, past Mum's oatmeal bread rising in the gold mixing bowl. Hope points up the street, but I can't see beyond the overgrown pine and juniper trees, the dogwood and the rhododendron bushes blooming around the end of our driveway, closing in around us. It feels like all of Cawood is right here in our yard, full of trees and pussy willows, chickens and swamp.

"Come on, Emily, now or never," Hope says from the top of the stairs. "Are you coming?"

"Yeah, are you coming?" Elizabeth Ruth asks. Hope's my oldest sister, then Sarah, Elizabeth Ruth, and me.

I reach around and pat along my shoulders until I think I find a bony lump right at the back of my neck which seems to grow bigger right under my fingers. Elizabeth Ruth sees me and says, mimicking Mum, "That's what happens when all that badness piles up inside — tchh, tchh, tchh." I don't want to be like old hunchbacked Mr. Kosik with his back so swollen up and hunched over with sins that his head is like a turtle's tucked into his chest. I'll go with my sisters, but I won't tell them anything. I follow Elizabeth Ruth into Hope's room next to the bathroom, where we'll confess our sins.

"We'll see who's going to heaven," Hope says, spreading the bathroom mat in front of the tub and draping a towel over the curtain rod of the bathroom window to block out the morning light. Then she stands in the doorway and nods, meaning she's ready for Sarah to come and kneel inside the tub to make her confession.

Hope shuts the door on me and Elizabeth Ruth sitting on the edge of Hope's bed, waiting for Sarah to finish confessing and kneel by the pillows we've set on the floor by the window to say her penance. Hope has a small paper plate of Ritz crackers on the windowsill. Afterwards, when it's my turn, Hope will take one of the crackers and say, "The body of Christ." I'll answer, "Amen," and stick out my tongue. Just like the Eucharist when we used to go to church, the Ritz will dissolve in the few seconds before I swallow it. Then I'll start laughing with them, covering my mouth, because we know we're not supposed to.

"Do you think she has any sins?" Elizabeth Ruth asks.

I shake my head.

"What is she saying, then?" She marches up to the door and puts her ear on it.

I don't know what Sarah could possibly confess. She never does anything wrong. I try to listen and hear only a murmur.

Water drips steadily from the sink and a housefly buzzes, banging its head against the windowpane. No one's going to find out what we're doing. Dad's in the garage, where he always is, working on a new invention, and Mum's nursing our newborn brother. When I saw them in the rocking chair, I thought that he looked just like one of those shriveled-up things in the huge pickle jars lined up at the traveling circus behind the Cawood elementary school. Hope paid a nickel for each of us to see them floating in the thick yellow water. Sometimes when I practice holding my breath underwater in the tub I can still see those ugly little things, curled up around themselves floating, some with their heads hitting up against the side of the glass. That was the last time we went to the traveling circus show. After that, we weren't allowed because, Hope told us, they were abortions, which is equal to murder in Mum's eyes. That's an absolute sin, the kind that's impossible to get rid of.

I hear the metal rings holding the shower curtain knock together and Sarah steps out of the bathroom quietly smiling, putting two fingers up, two, four. Two Our Fathers and four Hail Marys.

Hope's voice rises and falls as she sings from the bathroom, "Bluebells, bluebells, eevy, ivey overhead, Mum's in the kitchen making bread, Daddy's in the parlor, cutting off his head. How many chops did he receive?" She pauses, staring squarely at me and Elizabeth Ruth. "One, two, three, four, five, six, seven —"

"You're disgusting." Elizabeth Ruth interrupts Hope and steps quickly in to confess. Right away they're giggling, then the toilet flushes. I bet they're making up sins. I don't want to go in there. I can't talk. Why can't they understand that? I've heard them say to strangers, "She doesn't talk." I don't know why they don't tell themselves that.

I hold my breath. I can hold my breath longer than anyone I know. I can, until the sound of the ocean fills my ears. I do it until the braid running down Sarah's narrow back turns white. Everything turns white, pure white. If Mum saw me, she'd say, "Emily. Now stop that, Emily. You're going to pop a blood vessel if you don't watch out."

In no time Elizabeth Ruth has confessed. "Well, go ahead," she tells me, waving me in. They can't make me talk, I tell myself, they can't.

It smells of wetness and soap in here. The bathroom towel hanging from the curtain rod is glowing with a yellowish light shining through it like a stained-glass window. Hope is kneeling on the tiles outside the tub with her hands folded over the edge of the porcelain. It's my turn to step into the tub and fix the curtain so it is between us but I can still see Hope's blurry face. As soon as I kneel down I can feel the lump growing bigger on my back. When she touches her fingertips to her forehead, the center of her chest, to the left shoulder, then to the right in the sign of the cross, I do, too.

"You're supposed to say, Bless me, Father, for I have sinned. It has been however long since my last confession. I have done this and that and this and tell me what happened. So, go ahead. Confess," she whispers, her voice hard and serious through the plastic curtain. "Say something, Emily. You better. Remember Mr. Kosik.

"Why'd you stop talking?" Hope pauses, bending her head lower. "You have to say something. If you ever want to be normal again, you have to talk sometime. Go ahead, Emily. Confess."

It feels like there are fingers pressing around my neck. I can't breathe. Where are you, Ham? William Cunningham. I never want to go back there — to the island.

I think if I hold my breath long enough, I'll never have to talk again. I suck in the dark damp air all around me. I close my eyes tight enough to squeeze all the light out, making everything black then white and the pictures start showing inside my head. I can't stop them. We were driving down Beach Road, the blue-green water on both sides of us singing, *Row, row, row your boat, gently down the stream.* It all comes back so fast, I can't stop it. It was Dad's idea and we already had our bathing suits on.

"I saw kids younger than you jumping yesterday," he said and pulled the Oldsmobile into the sandy lot.

Dad, one of us called.

But he had already walked out to the bridge and was peering into the water below. Ham didn't want to go. "Come on now," Dad called.

"Get right over there," he said, lifting me over the guardrail. "There you go." The birds screamed from under the piling a few feet down, and below that, the water rushed by in white swirls. I tried to turn around. "Emily. Ready? I'm going to say one, two, three."

"Dad." I could barely hear Ham. His toes curled around the wooden edge. Then Dad said three.

He didn't jump with me. He was twisted and falling. The water was pulling me away from Ham. I saw a flash of red on his face before he hit the water.

Take your head out of the water, Ham, I wanted to yell. Nothing came out of my mouth, but a sound came out of Dad, something between a howl and a bark. Dad's face was like one of those rubber masks pulled tight over his skin and his eyes were white. Then I couldn't see him anymore. The flapping and cawing of birds was all around me. Seagulls were flying out from under the bridge toward the light, toward Ham floating with his head down in the water. All I knew was that something was wrong.

He was my twin, my half.

Someone is shaking me by the shoulders. "She's holding her breath," Hope says, ripping the shower curtain open.

When I open my eyes, Mum is standing above me. "Stop it, Emily. Stop it," she tells me. "Just stop it. Hope, I told you, no more of this."

"Her face is purple," Elizabeth Ruth says, peeking in from behind the door.

"For heaven's sake, are you hoops?" Mum asks. Next thing I know, one half of me is being yanked up by Mum's good hand, her fingers like barbed wire under my arm.

"Everyone outside," Mum announces, pulling the towel down from the window, letting the sun pour through. The top of her dark hair and face shine. Hope catches one end of the towel. Holding the two corners, she waits for Mum to get the towel between the stubby finger and thumb of her small hand. When their fingers meet at the corners, they smile to each other somewhere beyond me. Hope takes the corners and Mum takes the middle loop of the towel. Just the towel between them, they are so close they must be able to see themselves in each other's eyes.

I want to be that close to Mum.

"Praise the Cord," Hope says sarcastically to us following her downstairs. The embroidered banner in the hallway is supposed to read "Praise the Lord" but the *L* looks more like a *C*.

"Outside, everyone," Mum repeats from the top of the stairs. "Everyone outside. It's the best day I've ever seen." She's always saying it's the best day she's ever seen.

Only one square on Mum's calendar hanging in the broom closet is marked in July and that is today, July 4, 1974, Independence Day. One thing I do every morning is check the calendar. July's photo of Cawood is taken from an airplane and shows all of Main Street from the new Friendly's to Star Savers to the steeple of St. Peter's Church to Donut Haven. On the map, Cawood is just a pinpoint, less than a thumb from Boston, but on Mum's calendar, Cawood is absolutely huge.

"Crappy Cawood," my oldest brother, John, says, passing by.

I run outside, away from all of them, to the back of our house, where the loose threads of pussy willow tickle and scratch my throat. When I get to the muddy stream I jump from stone to stone until I am across. I put my arms around the reddish brown trunk of my cherry tree peeling sideways in strips and shimmy up to where there is a flat space in the crook of the branches bursting with cherries. The cherries are like small stones, egg-shaped, hard, and deep purple. They've never grown to full size, all pulpy and sweet, like they're supposed to. A sparrow dives through the sky, swooping down to spy on me, reminding me of what I've done. The flutter of its wing tips touches the edges of my ears.

My younger brother Luke yells and hoots Indian cries, runs and swipes at the clean towels, sheets and pillowcases, underwear and socks hanging out to dry on the clothesline in our backyard. All twisted by his boxing fists, the linen looks like ghosts floating back and forth. The sparrow has disappeared.

I can see our whole backyard from here. Elizabeth Ruth pulls her T-shirt up over her head and flings it to the ground. The sun glows off the white of her chest and belly. Even though she's only thirteen, two years older than me, she's much taller and curvier, and already has pink tips. I don't take my eyes off her as she marches over to where the wildflowers and bramble grow along the edge of the swamp and plucks off the heads of two black-eyed Susans which she places on her tips.

I slide down from my tree to get closer to her. I stand like she is with her elbows jutting to the sides as she holds the flowers there. As soon as Luke sees her, she drops the flowers and runs through the tall grass in the vegetable garden yelling, "Betcha can't catch me." He yanks a pair of Dad's boxer shorts off the clothesline so hard the clothespins pop in the air.

Elizabeth Ruth shrieks and runs faster as he chases her. My heart jumps. I want to stop her from breaking the rules before she gets us all in trouble. When she gets to the chicken coop, she turns around, hitching her thumb inside the top of her cut-offs, swirling her hips around and around like mixing beaters. "Gimme that," she yells to Luke, who has her shirt in his other hand. He throws it up on top of the wire meshing of the coop.

Fluffing her clipped feathers and tossing her white-crowned head, Gertrude lifts herself off the ground and floats a couple of feet beneath where Elizabeth Ruth's T-shirt landed. Gertrude, the only chicken we've ever named, is our best layer.

The whistle sounds.

A burning heat sears through me. There is Dad, holding the whistle strung around his neck. He walks backward, cutting a long line into the wood chips with the heel of his work boot. If there's one thing about Dad, it's that he always thinks he's right. "Am I right or am I right?" he says to us when he's in a good mood, which isn't now. We run for the lineup because we have to. Dad likes everything in top order. I stand up as straight as I can, combing my hair back and wiping my nose with the back of my hand. Elizabeth Ruth is shaking, goose bumps running up and down her. I feel them too, going up and down me. When I glance at her again, I notice something else. At first I think the sun is playing tricks on me, but her eyes are bright blue, like Ham's. I can't stop looking at her.

We fall into our places, all six of us in order: John, Hope, Sarah, Elizabeth Ruth, me, and Luke. Dad drags his eyes over us, with our toes on the line, arms at our sides, shoulders back — all except Elizabeth Ruth, who has to hunch over herself, her arms folded across her chest to hide herself. Luke still has Dad's boxers bunched in a ball in his fist. Dad takes a last gulp of beer before he sets the can on top of the chicken coop. As soon as he turns his back, Hope arches her body to us, zippering and unzippering her imaginary fly, then pointing to Dad. Her arms fall straight against her sides when Dad faces us again. His zipper is down. His eyes are black circles and his whistle dangles around his neck as he marches in front of us, staring at us like he's trying to figure out who we are, who he's getting back into order.

The chickens are squawking and flying under their cover, fluttering across the water vessel, blowing the dust everywhere, to get back into their nests in the chicken coop. I don't know why we have to have chickens, nobody else does. Hope says nobody in the suburbs has chickens. We all hate them, except Dad, who eats his eggs every morning and says to Mum, "We'll never have to buy eggs again." Mum just nods.

The can of Busch beer shimmers from the top of the chicken coop. I wonder what he's going to do next. Sometimes when I look at Dad, I see him like he was right after he made the Magic Rose. He was written up in the papers and on TV and everything. Mum bought donuts and we stayed home from school to watch him talk about the Magic Rose on one of those morning talk shows.

"Our next guest is Donald Stone, inventor of the Magic Rose. If any of you don't know what this is yet, the Magic Rose grows overnight *and* changes color depending on — well, what else? Love. On how you love the person you give it to!" the woman explained, holding one of the Magic Roses for the audience to see. "Ladies and gentlemen, please welcome, Donald Stone."

Then he was walking across the silver screen in the same gray suit and tie he wore every Christmas as everyone applauded. "There he is!" Luke ran to the set to wave to him.

"Donald, I've got to tell you, when I got the Magic Rose from my husband, I didn't know what to expect. I have to confess, I didn't actually think it was going to work." Titters of laughter came from the audience.

"I gave it a few drops of water before I went to sleep, as I was instructed, and lo and behold in the morning there was my perfect white rose — which I have brought to show you. Here it is, so everyone can see." She held it up to the audience, who hollered and whistled. "And white is the color I want, right? White symbolizes pure true love, isn't that right?"

"That's what they tell me," Dad answered.

There was a pause then.

"I've been told," the woman continued, "that red is for passion, blue constancy, and yellow happiness." The truth is, they didn't start out as love roses, but that's what they turned into.

"Why doesn't he wave to us?" Luke interrupted. "Why doesn't he say hi?"

We laughed and told him to get out of the way.

"Shh," Mum said.

"Why isn't he saying anything?" I asked.

"He said something," Mum said.

"Why isn't he saying anything now?" Ham asked.

Dad nodded. He didn't look very big on the screen. Maybe it was the way he squeezed his hands so tight to his body, or maybe his suit was too small. His face looked frozen.

"Why isn't he saying anything?" I asked.

"He said something before," Mum said.

"Why isn't he saying anything now?" Ham asked.

"Shhh."

"I guess you're not going to give any secrets away."

"Oh, no." When Dad shook his head, his face went red.

They had to stop for a commercial break and then they must have run out of time, because when they came back, Dad was gone. The show kept going and we all sat around the TV, waiting for him to return.

"Well, that's too bad," Mum said.

Dad was famous then. Some people even said the rose grew right out of the palms of their hands. But no one buys the Magic Rose anymore. Now Mum says, "Be good children. Your father works very hard." Then she asks us, "Do you know what the secret of a happy person is? To be thankful for what you have. And we have everything we need."

Hope whispers to Sarah and Elizabeth Ruth that the hospital bills haven't been paid and Mum pretends not to hear her. And Dad stays in the garage most of the day trying to invent something new. When he comes out, his mouth smells like beer and his hands are fists. Like now.

Dad stops in front of Elizabeth Ruth and drags his eyes down to her little tips. "For crissake, Elizabeth Ruth, why don't you have a shirt on?" Dad's bulldog Bud sniffs around his legs.

Elizabeth Ruth shrugs and answers, "I don't know."

"Well, you better find out." Dad bends down to rub the loose skin under Bud's chin. Everyone can see the light blue cotton of his boxer shorts behind the open zipper. "Elizabeth Ruth and John, stay right where you are. The rest of you can go find something to do." He sweeps us away with a swish of his hand.

I run as fast as I can to watch Elizabeth Ruth through the bay window in the laundry room, where Dad's tan work pants are hanging to dry. I push them aside so I don't have to stand between the stiff legs. The curve of Elizabeth Ruth's back glows in the sun as her head bobs up and down with her crying. If I were her I'd put something over my face, like my hands. She's just supposed to wait there.

Dad hands John the chicken catcher with the wooden handle and sharp metal hooks on the end to pull Elizabeth Ruth's T-shirt off the top of the chicken coop. After he tosses it to her, Dad nods to him, telling him he can go.

Almost tripping on a baseball bat as he walks away, Dad picks up the bat by the thicker end, steps back, and grimaces as he hurls it far into the pussy willows. Mum says it helps her when he gets so angry to remember the photograph of their wedding day, which she claims makes him look like Cary Grant. So I try to imagine the photo with Dad, smiling and tanned in his black tuxedo, with a lily of the valley in his lapel. I see Mum being thankful for everything as she stands beside him holding the umbrella over their heads. Behind them the rain pours down so hard it is like bright white sheets.

The hollow willow stems break to catch the bat. Bud trots beside Dad, following him wherever he goes.

Elizabeth Ruth has to stand there on the line until Dad comes back. Across from her, a small chicken claws a hole in the dirt, the dust rising and falling in the hot air. I know she hates chickens so much that she keeps scratching her legs and arms as if that'll get the chicken smell and feather dust off of her skin. "Sometimes," she told me one night in our room, "I dream I am swimming in the ocean. I must be on my back because I can see the clouds floating by. Then they start floating down toward me in the water. And I'm naked. I don't have anything on. Then the clouds start falling from the sky. When they get closer, I see they aren't clouds. They're chickens, the clouds have turned into white chickens. They try to land on me and peck me. Whole pieces of me. And their claws stick into me. Yuck." In the silence, she whipped her face toward me and said, "Sometimes I hate telling you things." Then she shivered, holding and rubbing herself around the back like she's doing now.

Mum comes up to the bay window of the laundry room with my new brother. "What on earth did she do now?" Mum asks out loud. She unbuttons her blouse and holds up her breast with her small hand, the first finger like a claw and the rest of her fingers shrunken to reddish stubby things. I stand on the tips of my toes to see more, but all I see is a wet milk stain on the front of her blouse. I don't even mind that her hand is like a lobster's. No one thought she'd have another baby, except Dad. He's the one who wanted it.

Her wraparound skirt hangs loosely on her thick waist. Below her knee is a tiny hole in her stocking, perfect and round. I want to put my finger there on her skin. Mum's so taken by the spitting and sucking noises the baby is making, she gazes into his face, murmuring, "Nothing is going to happen to you, no. You just stay right here.

"Emily," she says, suddenly noticing me, "it was hot like this at Ham's funeral. Remember?" She's not looking at me anymore.

"Before we even got there, we were all sweating. I never should have worn that blue dress. Everyone could see the sweat stains under my arms. How disgusting. I don't know what made me put that thing on, but I really should have thought about it. Your father was worse off in the awful seersucker suit. The sleeves were too long." She sighs.

"There were so many people there. Your father kept saying, 'Look at them all. This is when people really stick together. They're all here for us. When's the last time you saw a crowd like this, huh?'"

Mum hasn't mentioned the funeral before. I don't remember her dress or Dad's suit or anything, except a strange feeling, burning through me like hot fluid, rising to the top of my head. And I remember Ernie, Dad's brother, came up behind Dad and put him in a choke-hold. He's much bigger than Dad and I thought he was going to suffocate Dad and I think Dad did too, because he broke down. Fell to the floor in a heap, I mean.

Elizabeth Ruth sees us in the bay window and waves. Mum waves with her good hand. "What on earth did she do now?" Mum asks again, then heads out of the laundry room.

I'm small for almost eleven and can still fit inside the dryer, where it's cool and no one will see me. I lay on my side, my cheek against the linty metal, with my chin tucked between my knees and my arms pulling in my shins. With the palms of my hands, I feel all around me, running my fingers over the curve of the metal in here full of dark shiny holes that remind me of the yellow beady eyes on Bud's sagging face. I think about how much I hate Bud. Ham wanted to get a dog, but Dad said it would be too much work for Mum. Now we have a new brother and a new dog, both with scrunched up faces.

My hand slides between my legs to where my cut is on the inside of my thigh. I pick at the edge, prying the hardened covering loose so I can slip my finger underneath, lifting the scab, waiting for the thin pain to run through me. I keep lifting and picking and digging into the scabby web until blood trickles down and my leg is throbbing.

The sharp blows of the whistle make me jump and hit my head on the curved top of the dryer. I push the door open and spill out into the silvery air. Something metal clinks. I grasp a clean silver coin, a buffalo nickel.

I'm the last one to get back in line. Even Elizabeth Ruth is there, dressed and quiet. My heart's beating so fast, I think Dad's going to hear it and make a new rule: no hearts can beat too fast. Feeling a tiny trickle of blood seeping down my thigh. I squeeze my legs together. I hold my breath. I clamp my top teeth to my bottom teeth and squeeze my stomach muscles as if water is pressing in all around me, as if I am swimming underwater.

Row, row, row your . . .

2

"Oh, for God's sake," Dad mutters, squinting and swiping his arms through the hot air. His heavy work boots kick up the dry dust of feathers and chicken shit inside the coop. The chickens scramble and flap away from him, flying onto the wooden rim of the U-shaped feeding trough partially filled with pellets, old lettuce, apple cores, and eggshells. The next time he uses the chicken catcher to pull in a chicken's feet and doesn't miss. His fingers, thick as leather, wrap around the chicken's neck and its clawing feet.

He has to duck and shift his broad shoulders from right to left to fit through the door of the coop. When a piece of wire catches on his shirtsleeve, he jerks his arm away, ripping the cotton material, leaving a tatter hanging on the snag of meshing. Hope grunts, smothering her laughter. Dad swings his head around, searching. Bud stares up at him, panting and wagging his tail, and yelps.

"That's right, we got 'em, Bud." Dad chuckles. He passes the chicken to John and says, "Go get this ready for your mother like a good kid." With his mouth open, Dad nods toward me. "You can help him, Emily." He clears his throat, a racking cough.

I'm afraid of Dad's open mouth like a black hole, afraid of what I remember. I slip the coin into my pocket, press it to my thigh. It is a ring of silver. *It is Ham.* Dad took me around the waist with his huge hands and threw me straight into the air. My birthday dress filled with air as I flew up and up. I was five or six. It wasn't until I was falling toward him that I got scared. He reached out his arms to catch me, but I thought he might miss. I thought I might fall into that dark mouth. But he was smiling and his hands were around me. Then he threw Ham into the air and I watched him, feeling like Ham was me and I was Ham. I turn up to the sky as if I'm going to see Ham flying into the air, then falling into Dad's arms, his heart still pounding like mine. Sometimes I think I wanted Ham to die and that's what happened.

The chicken fluffs up and squawks in John's hand. "Crappy chicken for supper again," John complains. I follow the back of his Converse sneakers around the house to the garage. Chicken legs, I think, watching him walk, swinging the chicken back and forth. Tilted on its side, a wheelbarrow lies at the edge of the vegetable garden. Inside it old potatoes are floating ruined in the rainwater that has collected from the storm two days ago. Eyes are growing all over the potatoes, bright green and as big as anything. It's as if they're watching summer grow closer around us, as if they can see everything.

It's cool in Dad's garage, where all the windows have been washed over with white paint. We go to the corner of the garage, where the butcher-block table is stained dark brown with blood. Beside it a metal trash barrel buzzes with houseflies and deer flies. Hope told me that every time a housefly lands, it throws up, so I am trying to dodge them as horses do, by stamping my feet to the ground and sweeping my ponytail across my back.

John places the chicken's head over the groove marked into the wood by the ax, pinning the body of the chicken by holding down its twisting legs. His lips curve up into a smirk when he says, "It's time. Somebody's got to do it." He runs his fingers through the brown-and-white spotted feathers of the chicken.

Dad has set two-by-four boards up on a trestle horse as a shelf for the tubs of a latest new creation. It began as a special heavy-duty laundry detergent and turned into Tiger Soap, its name written in fancy dark script next to an orange and black tiger roaring. In a balloon from the tiger's mouth, it says, "Grr. A mean, degreasing hand soap so tough no water is required for washing." Dad planned to sell it to auto mechanics and construction workers.

A couple of weeks ago, Dad came in before supper to show us how Tiger Soap worked. "Look, they're absolutely filthy," he explained, rubbing the sandy soap on his dirty hands, "but this stuff'll take off the worst kind of grease." He showed us the palms of his hands, then wiped the grit off with a dry towel, showing us the fronts and backs of his hands again. We formed a circle around him to inspect his hands. The Tiger Soap had cleaned most of the grime off except for the black trapped underneath his fingernails.

"Are they really clean?" Mum asked.

"Of course they are. Do they look clean to you, Sarah?"

"Yes, Dad."

"Elizabeth Ruth?"

"Yes, Dad."

"See," he said to Mum. "And I don't want anyone giving my secret recipe away. I think this is going to be the next big one.

"Am I right or am I right?" he asked us as he held his hands up to the light. Dad scrutinizes everything and everybody with his "tight eye," as Mum calls it.

The chicken escapes out of John's hands and is clucking and scratching and fluttering all over Dad's things, finally landing on top of the telephone that Dad installed after the Magic Rose. John chases the stupid chicken with one of Dad's old fishing nets, even though no one is supposed to touch Dad's stuff.

I know the house rules.

No touching Dad's things, no running around without a shirt on, no high heels, no makeup, no bikinis, no swears, no talking back, no playing inside, no TV, no music except when Dad plays it in the car, no visiting the neighbors, no milk except in cereal, because we spilled it so many times, no toys or anything left on the front lawn, no eating anywhere but the kitchen — unless Dad says so.

And no talking about Ham, not even saying his name.

Last fall Dad started making all these rules to get us back in order. The only rule he can't make is one to make me talk again. I'm never talking again. They should all know this by now.

Last September, during the second week of school, Mum asked, "Emily, why aren't you eating your cereal?"

"She's waiting for him," Elizabeth Ruth whispered and pointed. "Look, she has two bowls." Hope elbowed her.

"Did I ask you?" Mum asked Elizabeth Ruth.

"No."

"No what?"

"No, Mum."

"That's better."

"Did you really think she was going to answer you?" Hope asked Mum.

"Time for school," Mum said, dumping the uneaten cereal back into the box. "Hurry up, everybody, out to the car."

Mum went to the closet to get her coat. Dad was sitting in his office watching TV. She stood in the doorway sliding the raincoat over the sleeves of her nightgown. "What should we do about Emily, Donald?"

"About what?" he asked.

"About the therapist," Mum answered slowly. "Mr. Pease thinks Emily should see a speech therapist, remember?"

"I don't want them giving my kids any of that bologna."

"They said we had to. He's sending a form home today for us to sign."

"Don't sign anything," Dad ordered. "They can't make us do anything. They won't do anything. Emily. Emily, come here. Do you want to see a therapist?"

I shook my head.

"Okay, now tell me, when are you going to start talking again?"

I shrugged. Dad was slumped on his desk. The TV buzzed beside him. It was the woman who had interviewed Dad about the Magic Rose talking to someone new.

"The school called. Your mother's upset. Is that what you want?"

I shook my head. I was trying to hear who was going to be on the morning show Dad was on.

"Well, I want you to stop all this nonsense. There's no need for it, do you hear me?"

I nodded.

"Come on, Emily, we're late," Mum said.

The school sent forms home with me; the guidance counselors called and mailed forms. Then our principal, Mr. Pease, stopped by our house. After Dad talked to him on the front step, Mr. Pease drove away and didn't come back and then the calls stopped and the forms stopped coming.

No one said anything to me at school, not at first and not now. I started to feel like I had disappeared with him, until I heard them talking. I was hanging by my knees from the monkey bar with my back to them, huddled in a circle with their arms crossed, shifting their feet as they talked.

"Hasn't said a word yet," my teacher, Sister McCarthy, said. "Such a shame."

"I wouldn't stand for it in my classroom. I'd make her talk like everyone else and I will next year," Miss Osbourne said. "It's the only way."

"How? We've tried everything," Sister McCarthy said. Sister didn't call on me anymore for an answer, and she stopped pairing me up. Before I left each day, she'd put her hands gently on the top of my head and murmur a prayer.

"I wouldn't let her go home. She'd stay right there until she talked."

"You can't do that for the love of Mike."

"No luck with the therapist?"

"None. The Stones want nothing to do with him, and when he comes into the classroom, she won't even look at him."

"Mrs. Stone hasn't been in all year. She used to be so active. I feel so bad for her."

"It's a shame."

"It has to be terrible for them."

"It's such a shame."

"The older girls are doing fine."

"Good."

"Will she pass?"

"Her written work is fine."

They turned toward me, and I knew they were thinking what had happened was my fault.

"She never talked much before."

"It'll pass."

"You have to believe everything happens for a reason."

"Whatever that is, the good Lord knows."

"Yes," they all agreed. Then the bell rang. I could feel their eyes rolling over me.

"I don't know how she can hang there for so long every day."

A pounding filled my ears as the jungle gym, the running kids, the meadows all swirled in circles upside down.

"Emily! It's time, Emily!" Sister McCarthy called me. I tightened my knees on the bar, rocking myself, swinging my arms back and forth until they passed. If you don't say anything for long enough, people start to think you're not there.

"Emily, Emily." John is calling me. "Come here, Emily."

I'm standing over one of the tubs of Tiger Soap. It looks like gritty mud and smells old, like Nana's basement. No wonder it didn't sell, I think, pressing the top back down. I run back to where John is carefully holding the chicken's legs down on the butcher-block table, waiting for me with the chicken, its ugly brown-and-white speckled head turned to the side.

"Okay, Emily, just put your hands like this and say good-bye." I shut my eyes, letting him move my hand. The chicken's legs are hard twisted sticks beneath my hands. John keeps whistling the same tune as he practice-slams the blade of the ax down on the edge of the table. I open my eyes in time to watch the blade coming down, cutting through the bristly neck in one swing. I don't know if it's the ax on the table or the shine of the blade like the glint in John's eye, but I let go and the chicken's body flies up into my face like a ghost's. Feathers flap wildly on the headless body running across the air, right off the cutting table. I tumble backward onto the boards of ripe pine piled on a mound of dirt.

Arms over my head, I duck down, feeling its feathers brush madly across my hair, then I hear a thud.

John laughs and says, "Stupid chicken." I hope this doesn't mean bad luck. Its wings flutter up, then stop, then a fluff, then nothing. It's so quiet, I can hear my own breathing. This must be what Elizabeth Ruth feels like when she dreams of the clouds falling down on her like white chickens pecking at her.

"It's okay. It stopped moving," John tells me, smiling.

It's easy for him to chop off the chicken's feet. I can't look anymore, not even when he plucks. "You know what I'm gonna do?" he asks, and answers. "Get outta this crappy little town and go somewhere like California. Maybe I'll get a motorcycle and just drive. Two more years and I'll be free. I might not ever come back."

My mouth opens for a moment, then shuts. I want to ask him if I can have a ride on his motorcycle when he gets it. That lump in the very back of my throat swells up.

The body beneath the feathers is rubbery and tough. When I poke its pink belly, letting my finger bounce back, John says, "From running around too much," and lets another feather float to the ground into the pile between his legs. Later Mum will brush a gravy marinade with the basting brush over the body so many times we won't be able to see the red pokes in its dark body where the feathers have been pulled. First, though, she'll boil it until it's soft and she can remove any of the feather ends we missed.

There are white specks of dust like snowflakes stuck to the top of John's dark hair. He dumps the chicken's head, feet, guts, and feathers into the trash can, briefly scattering the flies through the still air before they settle back down on the metal lid. There is a faint echo of an explosion in the distance. When we step back into the afternoon sun, early fireworks are bursting over the horizon, melting into the sky like a giant blue moth spreading out its wings.

"Crappy Fourth of July," John says, then disappears.

Later that night, Mum stares out the window while the fat and gravy spatter around the chicken cooling in the sink. The long kitchen table is covered with the good cloth decorated with pink and blue elephants, their trunks linked in three pairs on either side. We've hung blue and red streamers and white balloons from wall to wall, but nothing feels like it should. Mum sticks a paper American flag on a toothpick into the topmost part of the chicken. She lifts the metal pan and carries it with a smile to the brightly lighted table. "We might as well pass everything out while we wait for your father," she says.

"Why don't we have any fireworks this year?" Luke asks.

"Why are you so stupid?" Hope asks back.

"Hope, if you don't have anything nice to say, don't say anything at all," Mum tells her.

"We wouldn't have anything to say to each other," John answers.

"Can we please just try to have a nice dinner?" Mum says. "Luke, pass the chicken."

"You eat it first," he says, passing the brown-glazed mound to Sarah. She turns her head, passing it to John.

"I kicked you last," Luke says to me, waiting for me to kick him back.

"I kicked you last," Luke says, again.

"No kicking at the table," Mum says, suddenly looking up from where she is sitting with her hands pressed together like she's praying. She peeks into the buggy where our brother is sleeping beside her. "For heaven's sake, we're supposed to be thinking of a name for the new baby."

"I know someone named Robert Robertson," Elizabeth Ruth says. "He's in my class and his father killed himself."

"Elizabeth Ruth, that's enough of that talk," Mum says.

"So, Mr. Levy's first name is Dick," John tells us.

"There are a lot of Dicks out there, John," Mum says.

"How about Dick Stone?" John says laughing.

"What's so funny about that?" she asks.

"How about Donald?" Luke asks and we all laugh, watching for Dad.

"I think we're supposed to be thinking of church names, right, Mum?" Sarah says, reaching for an ear of corn.

"Jesus?" Hope suggests, stabbing the chicken with her fork.

His office door swings open. I finger the buffalo nickel in my pocket. All of us sit up straighter in our chairs, watching Dad finish tucking his shirt in to his tan chinos, slipping his belt through the loops, and clinching it tight. He's wearing his drinking face, dull yellow and all emptied out. "Hi, baby," he says to Mum.

He sways slightly side to side, as he leans up on his toes to reach into the cupboard, beyond the cornflakes and Quaker oats, past the Star Savers raisins and Bisquick to his bag of miniature Milky Way and 3 Musketeers bars, which he slowly takes out along with the Star Savers peanut butter, clutching them all under his arm to carry back into his office.

It's all so funny, I can't help it. Something like a grunt or a belch explodes from my mouth. They all stare at me like they're waiting for me to say something else. Even Dad, with the jar of peanut butter stuck in his armpit and the candy in his hand, turns and stares. I wonder if he's going to open the Star Savers peanut butter to spread on his Milky Way and find SHIT written underneath the peanut butter lid like he did before.

I watched Ham open the lids as fast as he could in Star Savers while Mum was shopping and write SHIT with black marker, then twist the lids back on. We were eight, hiding behind the Doritos, waiting to see who bought a jar. Mum bought one.

"Oh, for God's sake," Dad cried out at the breakfast table. "Baby, look at this, for crying out loud."

When Mum held the lid out in front of her to read, Luke sounded it out, "Shit."

Hope snorted.

Mum cried, "Oh, for heaven's sake."

Dad snatched the lid back from her. In one hand he held up the lid and in the other he held the banana he was going to spread on his toast with peanut butter. "First thing on Sunday morning, this is a shame. It's indecent."

"You swear sometimes, too, Dad," Hope finally said.

"Don't be fresh, Hope," Mum said.

"That's different," Dad explained, eyeing all of us suspiciously. "Besides, I don't write them on peanut butter lids. Did any of you kids have anything to do with this?"

"Of course not, I just got it yesterday," Mum answered sharply, snatching the jar and lid. "Why don't we throw it away?"

"Are you kidding me?" Dad grabbed the jar back from Mum.

"It's probably contaminated," Mum said firmly.

"Oh no you don't. This is going right back to Star Savers." First thing on Monday Dad got a free case of Star Savers peanut butter, and his name was in the police report in the *Cawood Suburban Press*.

Remember, Ham? Here he is, I want to tell them, laughing through me, here he is. My half. My fingers tighten around the coin. I better be careful or everyone's going to know I have something of Ham's. I know I have to stop this rocking back and forth now because I can feel their eyes going from me to Dad and back.

"Emily," Mum says.

"What's the matter with her?" Dad asks, his face all tight lines now.

Ham lets go of me, and I finally stop and shake just my head, nothing. Nothing is so funny, Dad. Nothing.

With his candy bars and peanut butter under one arm, Dad shuffles out of the kitchen in his wool slippers. The ice in the tall glass in his other hand clinks as he walks. A minute later we hear the fuzzy hum of the television set in his office.

"Thank you, God, for all this good food You have given us," Mum says. "Amen." The basted chicken poked with fork marks sits in the center of the table. Butter is hardening over the roasted potatoes, and the corn on the cob has stopped steaming.

"Amen," everyone says automatically.

She passes around the plate piled high with ears of corn. Then there is a sudden dart of a sparkle in her eyes and she flies up, collecting all our cups of water with her good hand, cradling them against her chest with her small hand. Before Dad sees her breaking the rules, she spills the water into the sink, then returns our cups to our places to fill them with milk. I'm sure no one will spill her glass of milk tonight, like we did to get the rule in the first place. But if anyone does, it won't matter, because he's not here.

"No thanks, Mum." Sarah plants her hand over her cup. As always, she's on a diet. She announces, "I'm never getting married. Never ever ever."

Just as we finish drying the dishes, Hope and Elizabeth Ruth come running back from throwing the chicken into the garbage. Like the cat he has seen on the Purina commercial, Luke wriggles his body, stepping back one, two, then forward three steps, singing, "Chow, chow. Chow chow chow." Elizabeth Ruth joins in, the red, white, and blue paper flag sticking out from the back pocket of her cutoffs. Hope claps to keep the beat while both of them chow chow chow.

"Meow," Luke says.

I start clapping with them. I am making so much noise, my skin turns red, tingling.

"Look," Hope says, pointing at me.

I am floating outside myself. Something is happening to me.

Then we hear Dad coming, and everyone stops automatically and stares at something or picks up a book to read or finds something to do, as if we are playing musical chairs and he is the music ending.

But Dad just glances over at us and asks, "Anybody want to watch the baseball game tonight?"

In his office, we pull out the gallon cans of paint from beneath the workbench and spread them across the stone floor to sit on the round metal tops. Most of the cans are tan, the last color he painted our house. There is a coolness coming up from the floor in here that clings to my bare arms and legs. I hold myself around the knees, feeling tiny in the clutter of broken tools and brass lights and fixtures, and sailboat and plane models hung from the wooden beams along the ceiling. On his desk next to his bottles of aspirin and Tums, there is a vase holding a stem of dried purple lilacs, its blossoms like velvet dust. "I didn't know you liked lilacs," Hope says to Dad.

"We used to sell lilacs," he says, his head rolling back on his neck. "We'd make bunches of them in the morning. In the afternoon, we'd be on the sidewalk calling out, 'Lilacs for sale, lilacs for sale.'" His voice rises until he is almost singing. He leans forward when he cracks open a tall can of beer, and I can feel the cold spray of the beer at the same time as I feel the heat rising from him. In his shirt pocket, Dad keeps his bottle of white pills, the ones he started taking after the accident. Mum doesn't believe in taking drugs, but Dad does. I've seen them at the bottom of my chocolate shake, too. Three at a time. They don't taste like anything. His fingers are white, too, where they press around the can.

"For how much?" Hope asks.

The shadow of the model airplane falls across my knee as I hunch up over the paint can.

When I shut my eyes I see the same shadows crossing over my skin, but I was sitting on one of Dad's knees and Ham was on the other one laughing at the shadows racing across our legs. We never got too old for this one, did we, Dad? Until now. Now we're too old. It's almost our birthday. We'll be eleven. I think I've finally figured it out. Ham's coming back on that day.

"Row, row, row your boat, gently down the stream. Merrily, merrily, merrily, merrily, life is but a dream," Dad sang, his knee lifting up and down like a seesaw. He dropped his right knee so Ham shrieked and grabbed around his neck. It was my turn, then Ham's, then mine again, each time dropping closer to the stone floor. The blue stones wedged together are like water swirling around me. Is that you, Ham, flying across the room? Coming closer, it's almost our birthday, again.

I can't stop it coming. I always see Dad's thick hands coming closer, pressing so hard they turn white. The green-blue-gold water flowed into the lagoon where the fishermen were fishing and the seagulls were fighting over the leftover parts of fish. We were looking down from the bridge through Dad's fingers like a web spreading across the water. We turned ten that day last summer. I wanted Dad to look at me. I jumped.

"One, two, three," Dad counted and I, the show-off bird, jumped. I left Ham. He didn't want to jump. As soon as I hit the water I looked up and saw him falling twisted and backwards. I didn't mean to leave him. Then the water pulled me away from him.

The shadow of the model airplane is cutting back and forth across my knee, or else my knee is shaking. They're all screaming and clapping like the baseball crowd roaring off the TV. I need to find Ham wherever he is. I reach up to the ceiling to pull him down. He is the shadow passing by.

Turning from the ball game, Dad finally asks Hope, "How much for what?"

"How much for a bunch of lilacs?" Elizabeth Ruth answers loudly for Hope.

Dad tosses my brothers a bag of Georgia peanuts. John and

Luke are like cocks puffing out their blond breasts and ruffling their feathers, knocking each other off the paint cans, grabbing for the peanuts. They laugh, showing off in front of him. We're either showing off in front of him or running away from him. Folding his arms across his chest and leaning back in his cushioned easy chair, Dad laughs at them. "Who wants to make a bet?" he asks.

"I do," they yell. "I want the Red Sox. I call the Red Sox!"

Dad cradles his head in his hands and props his feet on his desk. He looks like the man in the cartoon Hope cut out of a magazine at the Cawood library. She keeps it in the back of her closet in a cigar box that reads, "Handmade Panatelas." A doctor, sitting just like Dad, pulls down a lever, which sends his patient straight through a trapdoor in the floor. Underneath it reads, "Too fucked up." Hope would be killed if Dad ever found it.

"Dad, how much did you sell the lilacs for?" Elizabeth Ruth asks louder for Hope.

"Oh, I don't know," he answers at last, looking at Elizabeth Ruth. "If we made ten bucks that would be a good day. We were hardworking kids all right."

Dad's yellow cheeks are becoming red like the rims of his eyes as he cracks open another beer and stores the empty one in the cardboard case by his feet. He walks around the scattered paint cans past us.

When he comes shuffling back, there is a glint in his hard blue eyes, white as the flash of white when the sun hits the ocean. He mutters, "Bitch." He says it soft and hard, leaning back in his office chair like he's talking to all of us. I know if Mum were here, her lips would be moving, saying little prayers between her teeth, enough to go around.

Ever since we came back to Cawood without Ham, Mum hasn't looked like herself. When she came home from the hospital after the operation, her arm was bandaged to the elbow, under her eyes was black, and her face was puffy and pulled tight like an inner tube.

Last Valentine's day, Mum's hand had blistered and blown up practically to the size of a grapefruit, but she wouldn't go to the doctor. Mum's friend Mrs. Duncan noticed Mum's hand at Star Savers. "You know I'm a nurse," she said, shaking her head and sighing, rolling Mum's red puffy hand in her own. "I'm going to tell you something right now. You shouldn't be food shopping. You should be in the hospital."

"I'll be fine. It's just a little cut," Mum said, pulling away her hand, hiding it.

"Oh, no. This is infected. I'll take you myself if I have to. Is Donald home?"

Mum shook her head. "He's out getting his supplies."

"You're coming with me. I'm a nurse, what else can I do?" Mrs. Duncan told Mum. "Girls, put back the groceries. I'll pick you up right out front. We're going *now*. Boys, come with me." She hooked her arm through Mum's good arm and marched out the door.

"Do you think she's going to die?" Elizabeth Ruth kept asking us, emptying the wagon, until Hope told her to shut up.

Mum didn't come home that night. Mum didn't come home the next night or the night after that either. We didn't go to school. Hope and Sarah heated cans of soup and made macaroni and cheese. Dad said Mum was too tired for visitors. He took John with him after dark, tied the bumper of the Oldsmobile with a rope to the bumper of his pickup, and pulled it home in neutral with John steering.

I started to wonder if Mum was ever going to come home. Hope told me she was sorry for every time she had played "Mum's dead," pretending Mum had died when she was only sleeping on the couch. I would hover over her, waiting for her to open her eyes, staring at her so long, I didn't know whether she was breathing or not. I screamed when her fingers fluttered, her mouth puckered, and she finally came alive. Sarah said she was sorry she had laughed when Hope did this. Elizabeth just cried, and every day Luke stared out the window, waiting for her to come back down Willow Street, where she had disappeared.

Luke was the only one who wasn't surprised when she came home. "Here she comes," he said on the third day, pointing out the window.

We surrounded her before she got out of the car. Her arm was bandaged to the elbow in white gauze, and under her eyes was black and blue. Luke dove into her waist. I touched the wrapping around her hand. "Home again, home again," she said, smiling at all of us. "I missed all my little monkeys."

"What'd they do to your hand anyway, Mum?" Hope asked, squinting into the sun.

"Come on, let her get some rest," Dad told us, clearing a circle around her, leading her inside. "She's tired."

One of the shutters outside the bedroom window had come loose and thudded against the clapboards of the house, rattling the room to its bones.

"Did it hurt?" Luke wanted to know. "Did they cut off your hand?"

Mum shook her head. "No, I'm just glad to be back home again." She put her good hand on top of her belly over the white bedspread. "Were you good children?"

"I was," Luke yelled.

"Did you help Hope and Sarah?"

"She made me do the dishes every night."

"Helped me go insane," Hope answered, carrying a tray of chocolate milk shakes and saltines with peanut butter and jam.

"How was the food?" Sarah asked. "Was it disgusting?"

"No, it was fine."

"Have a milk shake, Mum," Hope said. "Your favorite."

Dark strands of hair were sticking to Mum's mouth, and her lips were curved strangely up. It was her eyes that were different. I couldn't see my reflection in them anymore. They weren't looking at me or anyone. When I stepped closer, her eyes rolled up to the ceiling.

"I just have to rest my eyes for one minute," she said.

"Mum?" Elizabeth Ruth called. "Mum?"

She didn't answer Elizabeth Ruth. She closed her eyes, and that strange smile ran right off the side of her face onto the pillow.

That was last winter. Mum doesn't stay in bed all day now. She gets up early every morning, as soon as the baby starts crying.

Even though our new brother keeps her busy all day long, she has baked a Fourth of July pie with fresh strawberries and blueberries and a hill of whipped cream on top. She carries it into Dad's office and stands there holding it, with her bottom lip puckered up over her top lip. The apron over her wraparound skirt has the wet wrinkled print of hands. "A little pie?" Mum offers.

His hands holding his stomach, Dad keeps his eyes on the TV. Yaz is up, tapping the bat on home plate, circling the bat in the air around and around with his right hand, then gripping it with both hands and swinging it across the plate.

"Does your stomach hurt, Donald?"

Dad doesn't even glance at the Fourth of July pie she slides across his desk along with a pie cutter and a plate. He keeps holding on to his stomach and leaning back in his chair.

Mum leans against the wall. Beside her is a framed photo of the man Dad calls the best general America ever had — General Patton — smiling in his polished three-starred helmet, his hand resting on an ivory-handled revolver belted to his side. His tie is tucked neatly between the buttons of his shirt. Dad says Patton had the brains and the guts to fight the whole world.

"And it's a deep fly ball to center field," the baseball announcer's voice roars out. The ball game is over. We rise, the tops of the paint cans indented on our behinds, our palms filled with peanut shells, and leave Dad with his red, white, and blue pie. Mum's in the kitchen finishing the dishes.

"Your pie was really pretty, Mum," Sarah says and goes upstairs.

"I would have eaten it," John tells her.

"Me, too," Elizabeth Ruth agrees.

"You should go get it, so we can eat it right now," Hope says.

"He'll have some in a few minutes, and there'll be plenty left over for us," Mum explains.

"Why don't you get it now and he can have some when he's ready?"

"Listen, Hope, I just don't want a lot of trouble."

"I know, you just want a little peace and quiet, right?" Hope says, her eyes turning dark. "I'm going outside."

We all follow her out behind the clothesline, except for Sarah, whose sewing machine is going *clickety-clack, clickety-clack* upstairs. That's all she does since Mum gave her the old gray machine that looks like a submarine. It used to be her mother's and is always breaking down, but that doesn't stop Sarah from sewing all day and night.

The sheets, towels, and white johnnies Dad took home from the hospital without Mum knowing — she was having Owen — are blowing up and down in the night air. Mum said it was stealing. Dad said they were robbing us, the hospital bill was so high. The fireflies are lighting up the night. Hope brings us all mayonnaise jars. I lie beneath the stars spread across the darkness and find Canis Major and stare at him so long, it looks like he's chasing his dizzy tail, spinning around and around Little Dipper and Big Dipper.

Elizabeth Ruth skips with her jar, following the glowing light of the fireflies. "It's like catching a falling star!" she yells.

"I've got one! Look!" Hope screams out.

Luke trips into the wet night grass. "Hey, come back here, you." His voice trails off as he scrambles up again.

"I wish it would stay lit," Elizabeth Ruth says.

John doesn't play with us. He stares long and hard into the night sky, keeping an eye on everyone, because he's the oldest and the oldest always gets blamed if anything happens. Luke brings him a poster in dirt-smeared plastic he has found under some scrap wood in the garden filled with weeds and then squats like John, with his elbows resting on his knees.

Boom, boom, boom, the fireworks sound somewhere out past the junipers, the old elms, and sugar maples. The pretty yellow lights fall like stars into the black all around me. Just as I am about to make a wish, I see Ham falling twisted through the air toward the water where I am. I'm being pulled away from the light. I can smell him and hear him telling me something.

I turn to see Nixon's shimmering face drawn over with fangs and bloodshot eyes and poked through with dart holes on the unrolled poster. The booth to throw darts at Nixon's face at our carnival was John's idea. If you hit his eyes you won a pack of Bazooka, and if you hit his nose you won a peace pin. Otherwise you lost your quarter. In the dark it looks like the flesh has been ripped away to the bone of the president. Above the torn face of Nixon, his arms extended, giving signs of peace, the poster asks, in bold block letters, "Would you buy a car from this man?"

Even Sarah has left her basket of spools of thread, needles, and scissors to come outside, carrying an empty blue clay bowl. Luke is hitting rocks with a stick far into the woods. Each hit cracks the air open, splitting the night like the fireworks in the distance. The sky is so wide it seems it may swallow me up.

It's like I'm watching a TV show with all my brothers and sisters in it, but I'm on the other side of the screen, watching through the silver hum. I don't know how to reach them. They're right there in front of me, but I can't get to them through the screen. They don't see me, either. Bud sees me, though. He starts licking my face until I am wet with his slobber. *Stay, please, stay,* I want to tell him, running my hands over his soft fur, squeezing him too close. He yelps and slips away.

I follow my sisters inside. Dad has locked himself in his office, and Mum is rocking the baby in the cradle, pushing it back and forth. She smiles at us and asks, "Did you catch any fireflies?"

"Look," Elizabeth Ruth tells her, holding up the jar. She turns off the overhead light so we can see the yellow light of the fireflies darting around the jar, banging their heads against the side.

"I let mine go," Hope tells Mum, flicking the light back on.

"How'd you do, Emily?" Mum asks. "Did you catch any?"

I step closer, shaking my head.

Still rocking the cradle, Mum pulls me closer.

"Come on, let's go finish our game," Hope says.

"It's almost time to get ready for bed like good children," Mum calls after them.

"We're not tired," Elizabeth Ruth yells as she runs up the stairs, bolting to Hope and Sarah's room, where we left our Life game all set up.

"I don't care if you're tired or not," Mum calls up the stairs. She keeps one arm across my shoulder. Claw lady, I think. As she keeps rocking him, that look comes over her eyes. It's like I'm looking at her through a window, and I know then what she is going to talk about.

"Remember how many people came?" she asks. "I think all of Oak Bluffs was there. There were people standing all around the church, people I didn't even know, saying how sorry they were. And on a beach day, too. That's where we would have been if it hadn't happened. We were going to go to State Beach as soon as you got home. I had the cooler packed and everything with all your favorite things." Her words come out so slowly, like they are pulled taffy. She flicks her thumb at her blouse, like she's trying to remove a milk stain spread under her breast. It should have been me and not Ham, and I know that's what she and everyone else thinks.

"I thought I'd never go swimming again, that's what I told myself then. Now I dream about it all the time. Funny, isn't it?"

"Emily," Hope calls from upstairs, "we're skipping your turn."

Mum looks at me like she forgot I've been standing there. Then she says, "Go ahead, go play."

Hope's making a doctor's salary of $65,000, so she's ahead. I'm a travel agent and make only $12,000, but at least I didn't have to cheat, like Elizabeth Ruth did for the Superstar card. Then she went and put a blue peg in the driver's seat and said it was Leif Garrett.

"He's a little old for you isn't he, Elizabeth Ruth?" Hope asks. She doesn't answer.

Sarah opens the canister of saltines under the sewing machine, takes out a sleeve, and starts nibbling on the corner of a cracker. "Dad'd kill us if he found these in here," Hope tells her with her hands on her hips. "Does Mum know you have all these?"

"Yes, and who cares?" Sarah says, bending over the needle and flooring the foot pedal as she runs a piece of flowered yellow cotton across the sewing table. Her hair falls around her face. *Clickety-clack, clack.* "You can have some."

Bud is barking. A whooping noise floats from beneath the window. Someone is out there. The breath stops in my throat. I lean on the sill from the window by Sarah's bed to see Luke swooping in and out of the white johnnies floating up to the night sky. I see him and then he is gone.

From the woods, Bud trots past Luke and past the clothesline. The basted chicken we ate for supper is between his teeth.

It's not Ham. Something sinks inside of me.

"Youu-whoo," Mum calls through the night air. I can see her at the back door with her hands cupped on either side of her mouth.

"Your turn, Emily," Hope says.

The clickety-clack stops. They're all eating crackers. I keep leaning out the window, staring in the dark so they don't see my eyes swimming across my face.

"Emily, your turn," Elizabeth Ruth says. Someone unrolls the sleeve of saltines.

"You're here," Sarah says. She comes to the window to show me the plastic Life car with the pink peg stuck in the driver's seat. "Here you are."

3

Mum chops cucumbers and peppers into cubes to add with three dollops of mayonnaise to the tuna fish. "He's not going to bite you," John says to me, pushing my baby brother toward me. I guess the baby isn't as ugly as I thought he was. When John puts out his knuckle, the baby grabs it with red fingers like he's never going to let go. He makes sucking noises, pulling spit in and out of his mouth. Then he starts sucking John's knuckle with his gums. I put my knuckle in his mouth, too.

"Hey, John, are you your brother's keeper?" Elizabeth Ruth calls over from the living room. The *Bible Stories for Children* with glossy colored pages with gold trim around the borders is open on her lap. She laughs and slams the book shut, the yellow rays of light shooting all around Jesus.

"What are you talking about?" John asks.

Mum answers him. "God asked Cain, 'Where is Abel, your brother?' and Cain replied, 'Am I my brother's keeper?' Then God knew Cain murdered Abel. He cursed the ground Cain walked on and sent him away with a mark on his forehead." Mum closes her mouth tightly and firmly places the white bowl of tuna down. She smooths out her apron, then wipes the kitchen countertops to get herself in order before she fixes some stuffed eggs. Ask Mum anything about the Bible and she'll tell you. Even though we stopped going to St. Peter's Church, Mum keeps right on reading the Bible, praying, and thanking God for everything she has.

Dad comes in from the garage and places his hand on my shoulder. His eyes are glossy and red and his mouth smells sour, like vinegar and cigar smoke. I feel the weight of his hand there long after he passes.

"Guess who's going on vacation?" he asks us cheerfully.

"Um, us?" Hope asks.

"Yup, Martha's Vineyard, here we come, here we come," Dad chants. "Let's see a smile on this old sourpuss." He grabs hold of my chin in his strong fingers, tightening his grip to shake once good and hard. He's not going to let go until I crack one, so I focus on the bridge of his nose and force my lips to open. It feels like a hole is splitting apart my face, like someone else's face is smiling at Dad.

I can't go back there, I can't, I can't. I won't either. I'm sure Mum doesn't want to go either. After the Magic Rose, Dad bought a summer house in Oak Bluffs, by the lagoon. All Mum wanted was something close to the water and close to town. But I know she won't go back there. She keeps saying it's a good time to sell.

"Thatta girl," Dad compliments me. "That's my girl." This makes Mum happy, so she smiles up at him while she hits the hard-boiled eggs on the edge of the bowl, cracking the shells, which she carefully peels off with her thumb. A sliver of steam rises from the white egg. She's just thankful Dad's in a good mood tonight.

"What's for chow, Martha?" He calls Mum the wrong name, then squeezes her around the waist, lifting her up off the floor. Her Dr. Scholl's sandals clomp back on the floor. She keeps smiling even after he puts her down. Dad chants, "Martha's Vineyard, here we come, here we come," to the rhythm of "London bridge is falling down, falling down."

There is a picture of Jesus on the cover of the book with the Cain and Abel story. Golden light is shooting out of Jesus' open palms, His yellow hair, and shining smiling face. By the time I finish reading, I am so shaky I have to lock myself in the bathroom to check if I have a mark somewhere on myself. That would be proof that it was my fault. When I go to Martha's Vineyard, people'll say, "There goes Emily, the evil girl who killed her own brother. Let's kill her, too." I take off all my clothes and, using two mirrors, check my back, under my arms, my scalp, my neck, the bottoms of my feet, and everywhere else for a mark. I even check between my legs; I put my hand there and hold myself as hard as I can.

"Emily," Mum says from the other side of the door. I see Mum's face flash in front of me. Everything goes black. She's in so much pain, I wonder what happened. What happened, Mum? Why do you look so funny?

"It's suppertime," she says. "What's taking you so long?"

There I am in the mirror. If God were smart, He'd put the mark where everyone could see it. If I start to talk again, I'm going to ask Mum about this. "Mum," I'd say, "why did God let Cain live?"

I'd rather be Abel.

Right after supper, Mum takes the clothes off the line before the night air gets into them and Dad goes out to the garage to work on a new invention. I follow Elizabeth Ruth and Hope as far as the doorway to Mum and Dad's bedroom. Hope pulls the phone off the shelf of the night table on Dad's side and sets it on her lap. Her finger in the three circle, she dials it three times, and hangs up. Right away the phone rings back. This is supposed to test if the phone works or not, but they let it keep ringing and ringing until Dad finally picks it up in the garage.

Carefully, Hope lifts the receiver and listens for him to say, "Hello?"

Their faces light up when they hear his deep voice on the other end, and their hands fly over their mouths to keep in any laughter. "Hello?" Dad asks. "Hello? Who's there?"

Hope's face pinches in excitement. She puts her finger to her lips and hangs up the phone. As soon as it's hung up, she clenches her fist and says, "We did it!"

Elizabeth Ruth falls over laughing and rolling onto their bed.

"There's no way I'm going back to Martha's Vineyard," Hope declares.

"Me neither," Elizabeth Ruth agrees. "Why does he want to go back there anyway?"

"How should I know? Come on, get up," Hope says. "Fix the bed." Hope darts over to Mum's bureau, opens her top drawer, and yanks out one of her huge white nursing bras. The enormous cups flap open, making them both start to giggle. When Hope spots me watching in the doorway, she says, "I hate to tell you, but only people who talk can come with us."

"Yeah," Elizabeth Ruth agrees. I step back, pretending to stop watching them, but I want to be with them.

"I forgot one thing." Hope turns into their bathroom, the door held open with Dad's old work boot. She fishes through the bottom cabinet drawer, through the bottles of hair grease, Old Spice, Listerine, aspirin, and Pepto-Bismol, until she finally finds Mum's makeup wrapped in a plastic bag. I follow them into Sarah and Hope's room.

Sarah pretends not to notice them brush mascara on their eyelashes or roll the red lipstick on their lips, touching the corners with a folded piece of toilet paper. They dab the beige cream over the bridges of their noses, spreading it up to their foreheads and down to their chins. They work circles of pink gel up along their cheekbones. Hunched over, Sarah keeps her foot on the pedal, pushing the material right through the needle clacking up and down. Beads of sweat line her forehead like pearls.

Hope takes her clock radio with the Siamese cat face out of the closet. Last winter, when the Rileys moved out of the neighborhood, Hope found it in their trash. The glass covering the Siamese cat's face was broken. Since the Rileys never had kids, we guessed it belonged to Mrs. Riley, though it's hard to imagine a grown woman with a Siamese cat clock.

Hope plugs it in, holding it by her ear as she turns the dial. "Come on Elvis, give me Elvis. But I'll take the Beatles or the Rolling Stones, if I have to." She settles on a slow, cool song about the summer wind blowing in.

Elizabeth Ruth takes off her shirt to slip on Mum's bra with the metal snaps and pointy cups that seem to swallow her chest. There is a knock on the door. "Is everyone decent?" Mum calls in.

"No," Elizabeth Ruth yells, sliding the bra down over her knee and under the bed. "I mean, just one minute." Hope laughs, then remembers her face. She grabs the baby oil to rub all over her face, smearing the black mascara down her cheeks. Hope yanks the plug of the Siamese cat radio out of the wall and slides it under the bed.

"Here," Sarah says to Hope, tossing her a scrap piece of cloth printed with tiny yellow flowers. "It's just Mum."

"Well, the less she knows, the better," Hope mutters.

Hope wipes her face in a few swipes, then calls out to Mum, "Come in."

Elizabeth Ruth, who has smeared baby oil over her face, sucks in her breath when the door opens. Mum pokes her head in. "Does anybody know anything about the phone?" she asks.

We all look at Hope. "No," she answers quickly. "Did something happen?"

"Dad said someone keeps hanging up on him. He wants to change our number now. Did you hear the phone ringing? For heaven's sake, Elizabeth Ruth, what's all over your face?"

"Um, baby oil. I'm conditioning my face."

"I'd say so." Mum shakes her head at Elizabeth Ruth. "Just don't make a big mess."

"I won't, Mum."

"John, Luke," Mum shouts as she closes the door, "come here. I want to talk to you."

As soon as Mum leaves, Hope and Elizabeth Ruth grab each other, rolling on the ground and snorting and laughing. I want to roll on the ground and laugh and do that, too.

I want to belong to something. But when Hope springs up at me, grabbing me around the ankle, I stand stupidly with my mouth wide open. A sound rises through me like a bubble, but before it comes out of my mouth, I breathe in and clamp my mouth shut.

"Come on," she says.

"Do something," Elizabeth Ruth says.

They stare at me, standing there, swallowing the air.

The next morning, Dad decides he's going to take us to Sears to get some bathing suits for our trip to Martha's Vineyard or the Sound, as he calls it. We didn't get to go school shopping this year, so Dad feels that we should at least get new suits. He orders all the girls into the Oldsmobile. I hate driving in the car with him. Sarah has one window because she is the one who gets carsick, though she never actually throws up, and Elizabeth Ruth has the other window. I have to sit in between them so I don't try to climb out the window again, like I did after the funeral. I was in the front seat with Mum. At first she didn't see me climbing out — it happened so fast.

I lurch forward against the back of the front seat, grasping onto the slippery vinyl seat on either side of me before everything starts turning over and in on me.

"All set there, Emily?" Dad asks.

I nod.

"One of these days, you're going to talk to us, aren't you, Emily?"

I nod again. My sisters cover their mouths with their hands to stop laughing out loud.

Sometimes I forget the rest of Cawood exists at all until I see all the houses spread out before me. Next to us on the other side are the Coopers, who are in Florida almost the entire year, which is probably why Dad likes them the best of everyone on our street. The Rileys used to be next. They were our favorite. Every August, when the Rileys lived here, Mrs. Riley used to let us pick the blackberries running wild all over their backyard. Since Mrs. Riley couldn't have children, she liked us to come by as much as we wanted. Thinking about the smell of those blackberries and the heat they spread through the kitchen as they cooked with sugar makes my mouth water. This August we'll have to go extra early, before Dad gets up to eat his hot oatmeal and three boiled eggs, and we have to get in the lineup. On the way over, we'll wear the pots we use to collect the berries on our heads. "Potheads," John will say.

The For Sale sign planted on their front lawn is gone. Dad drives slowly, adjusting the radio dial. A slinky black cat is making its way between stacks of cardboard boxes piled up on top of each other on the sidewalk in front of the Rileys' house. "Look" — Hope points — "someone finally moved in."

"Probably another senior citizen," Sarah says.

"They're all older than the hills," Mum always says. Since the Rileys moved, Mum is the youngest one on the street, and Mr. Kosik is definitely the oldest.

The O'Dells are across from the Rileys on the left. They haven't been out to eat at a restaurant in twelve years, all the time they've lived here, not even Friendly's. They're old, at least forty, and spend all their time fixing the garden that takes up their whole backyard with rows and rows of every kind of flower there is. Dad says they're crazy.

The Lawtons are next to the O'Dells and on the same side, and Dad doesn't like them either. A few weeks ago when we were driving somewhere, Dad told us the Lawtons were atheists and not to go near their house. "What are atheists?" Luke asked.

"Someone who doesn't believe in God," Hope answered.

"Pagans, that's who," Dad muttered.

"What are pagans?"

"Someone who lives only for pleasure," Hope answered.

"What's wrong with that?" Luke asked.

"'What's wrong with that?' Are you kidding me?" Dad breathed hard.

"Shhh," Mum said. No one said anything.

"How much are we paying for St. Mary's?"

"He's only in first grade for heaven's sake," Mum said.

"Just answer the question," Dad told her.

"We don't even go to church anymore," Hope said under her breath.

"What?" Dad swung around. "What was that?"

No one answered him. Hope started using the word *pagan* whenever she could after that. "I'm going to be a pagan when I grow up," she'd say, "at least I'll enjoy myself."

Past the O'Dells' is an empty lot and then Mr. Kosik's house. The engine purrs and the wind brushes through the windows as we slow down near his house. We all look for Mr. Kosik, but see nothing. Dad whistles through the chewed cigar in his mouth to a piano song playing on the radio. The sky is so blue, it's almost purple.

Dad drives fast on 128 north. It seems to get anywhere from Cawood, we have to take 128. When we get to Sears, we find the sports department right away with its spinning racks of one- and two-piece marked-down suits. I don't see any other girls shopping in here with their fathers. Some of them stare at Sarah the way girls do when they think another girl is prettier than they are. Sarah already has a navy Speedo held up against her body. "This one is good for me," she decides. She hates taking her clothes off, same as me.

"You better try it on to make sure," Dad tells her, stepping forward. "These cost a lot of dough."

Dad looks at the saleswoman and asks, folding his arms over his chest. "It's better to try on the suits, isn't it, Miss?"

The saleswoman stops pressing the register key and agrees, nodding. "They're nonreturnable."

"All right, everyone in there. I want to see all the suits before I buy them." Waving at us with both hands, he herds us into the dressing room. We've all chosen navy Speedos to try on, except Elizabeth Ruth who takes a red one.

The lady who is stationed at a chair in front of the dressing room gives us each a plastic ring that has the number one written all around it. "I'm sorry, no men can come in here, sir," she tells Dad, pinching her lips and resting her knitting on her lap. As she raises her hand to stop him, her ball of yarn drops and unravels on the floor.

"They're *my* daughters." He half-laughs at her, scowling, pushing his hands deep into his pockets. "I need to see if their suits fit or not."

"Well, you'll have to wait now, won't you, sir, because men aren't allowed in the women's dressing room."

Dad doesn't budge. It gets so quiet, we can hear the hum of electricity.

She ravels the loose yarn back around the ball, adding, "Or I'll have to call security." Dad mumbles goddamn something or other under his breath as we march past him into the dressing room stalls.

I pull my curtain all the way shut and stand in front of the mirror, holding my suit. When I peek beneath the half-wall of my stall, I see Elizabeth Ruth's feet in the dressing stall next to mine and Sarah's across the way. I double-check that my curtain is all the way closed, then slowly drop my shorts. There are tan marks on each leg where my shorts come to, making the tops of my legs feel fat and ugly and white. I put my legs through and pull the suit up fast. The edges of my underwear show through. I got the same size as Sarah so my suit would be nice and baggy in the stomach and in the chest and never cling to me again.

The air-conditioning in here rides up my legs. I stretch my suit tight across my chest, a clamminess creeping over me. Shivering, I watch myself swoon in front of the mirror. I am freezing.

The hallway of the hospital was air-conditioned, making my suit stick to me. Outside seagulls were screaming and I had to remember where we were. Vineyard Haven, where the hospital was. We passed it all the time. We weren't supposed to be in there. What were we doing? I was trying to find out where Dad went with Ham. Dad held him the whole way in the backseat of the car while I sat up front with the man. I couldn't see Ham's face, only the white of his back and his arms and legs hanging limply around Dad.

"Can't you go any faster?" Dad shouted from the man to me. "Turn around, Emily. Stop looking at him. God help us. I'm begging You — if You're there, help us."

I thought He heard Dad because then Dad stepped out of the

car and began running and Ham's legs and arms flapped up, slapping Dad's sides and his head rolled to the side.

The man who had driven us here, though, rested his forehead on the steering wheel and shuddered. It wasn't until the first wave of cold air hit me in the hospital that I knew something terrible had happened.

One of the nurses wrapped a blanket around me and sat down beside me until Dad came back. She got up to give him her seat. But Dad didn't sit down and Ham wasn't there. He leaned up against the wall and put his face in his hands. He didn't see me when I waved to him. My suit clung to me. Then the doctor was there at Dad's elbow. "Just a couple of questions," he said, holding Dad up like a rag doll.

Dad answered everything until the nurse got to the questions about health insurance. "You don't have any?" she asked.

"No."

"Nothing?"

Dad shook his head.

The woman tapped the head of her pen.

"Come on over here, Emily," Dad said.

"Can you tell me what happened today?" Her thick brown lips moved slowly as she talked.

Dad's voice sounded like the TV. "They were holding hands about to jump off the second bridge."

"The second bridge? Where is that exactly?"

"Beach Road going to Edgartown. The kids are always jumping off it."

"Yes, continue, please."

"She just jumped" — he looked at me — "without him and he must have lost his balance or gotten scared. He fell and then tried to turn and grab the ledge of the bridge." Dad reached up to show the nurse how Ham grabbed onto the bridge, then he turned and covered his face with his hands. Dad's hands fell to his sides and he jerked his face up at the chin from the impact with the imaginary bridge. "Oh God, oh God, oh God, where were You?"

Her pencil scratched words onto the paper. One of the doctors passing by the desk said, "She needs shoes." I shivered like I'm doing now.

Hope flings my dressing room curtain open, sticking her face in. "Fit?" she asks, then right away answers herself. "It's hanging off of you, what size is it?" She examines the tag on the back of the suit. "Oh brother." She shakes her head at me like I'm an idiot and swishes the curtain shut.

Then I hear Hope yank another curtain open and say to Sarah, "You didn't even try yours on?"

Elizabeth Ruth struts toward us, staring back at herself in the three-sided mirror on the wall at the end of the rows of dressing rooms.

"Who do you think you are, Miss America?" Hope calls. Elizabeth Ruth throws her short hair back and parades back into her dressing room, humming along to the soft music coming out of the speakers above.

"Shhh." Sarah puts her finger to her lips. She whispers to Hope, "I'm too fat to try this on here."

At first I think Sarah must be joking because she's the thinnest person I know. She's almost perfect. I wish I looked like Sarah, but I know I never could when I'm always gobbling up tablespoons of peanut butter and slices of Wonder bread and finishing everything on my plate at supper. Sarah rolls whatever she can't eat into a napkin or else Mum finishes it, because Sarah has a stomach cramp or a headache, or something.

"It's true," Sarah repeats.

"Oh, very funny," Hope blurts out after a short pause, pulling Sarah up by the hand.

When I stretch the suit tight across my chest, my baby-points barely show through the nylon material. I wish they would stay this size because I don't want to look like the woman in *Playboy* that Hope found under John's mattress. That woman had the biggest breasts I've ever seen and a big head of blonde hair piled wave upon wave, the same honey color as the rug of hair inching between her legs. I hope I never look like that.

Dad paces back and forth along the counter even while he pays for our suits with crisp new twenty-dollar bills that he tosses next to the register as if they're nothing. We know this is a lot of money. We see Mum adding up everything in her head at Star Savers, then putting back all the extras. We see Mum writing the checks on Sunday afternoon, sucking in her breath, saying tchh, tchh, tchh to herself. Dad glances over at the dressing room where the dressing room woman is whispering and pointing at him. He mumbles something else under his breath, but I can't hear what because I'm standing far enough away, hoping that no one knows I'm with him.

He hurries out of Sears carrying the paper bag of Speedos, and we trail behind him. People stare at us when we walk past them. At first I think they're looking at a mark on me, but their eyes follow Sarah. She is so thin and so beautiful. Sarah pretends not to notice.

By the time we get to the Oldsmobile, Dad is sitting on the front seat, leaning forward clipping his fingernails into a pile next to the car. His whistle has slipped out of his shirt pocket and hangs like a beam of silver in the sun. Dad drops the nail clippers into his shirt pocket with the whistle, reaches over to the glove compartment, and pulls out a bottle of Tums, which he opens, tossing the colored tablets right out of the bottle into his mouth. He caps the bottle and shoves it into his pants pocket as he stands to stretch. "I'll be right back, kids," he says. "Don't talk to anyone. Keep the car doors locked."

We watch him get smaller and smaller, then disappear into the Chinese restaurant across the street with the neon sign flashing "Sun Island." Somewhere church bells are ringing into the summer air.

"Does he expect us to suffocate?" Hope asks, opening the front door and sticking out her legs.

"Did you hear him?" Elizabeth Ruth asks. "I think he called the woman in the fitting room a jackass."

"Who's the jackass?" We explode in laughter.

"I didn't even want a stupid bathing suit," Sarah says.

"He acts like he's giving us a million dollars or something," Hope says.

"Mum would be so mad if she knew he cut his fingernails in public," Elizabeth Ruth says.

"I'll give you five dollars if you go over to Sun Island and tell him we want to go," Hope says.

"Let's see the five dollars," Elizabeth Ruth answers.

"Emily, you do it." They laugh. "Go tell Dad it's time to go. Tell him we're never going back to Martha's Vineyard. We know you can talk, Emily. Tell him he's a jackass."

If I said something now, I'd be like them. But I can't talk. If Ham were here, I would, I tell myself, closing my eyes in the sun, listening to them laugh. When I wake up, everything will be better.

Elizabeth Ruth starts singing that song playing in the dressing room, "I'm as a free as a bird now," and I remember when I heard it before.

Ham was there. When was it? It was fall, I know that. The leaves were red, orange, and yellow and I know it was Sunday because we always went to Blue Hills on Sunday. We were going south on 128. *Freebird* was playing on the radio, and we were all singing along until Dad started yelling at the car in front of us for going too slow in the fast lane and so Mum turned the radio off.

He pulled the Oldsmobile into the middle lane and shot

around the car going too slow, the horn blasting, "Goddamn lady drivers!"

"It's a man, Dad," Ham yelled, waving at the old man in the Volkswagen bug.

"Well, he drives like a lady," Dad shouted back. His mouth was clenched and his face went red. This was what always happened when Dad drove — unless he was drunk.

In the front seat, Mum turned to us. "I have an idea," she said. "Let's play the silent game." Nobody said anything. "Ready? Set, begin." In her flowered print blouse, she leaned her head against the window and sank into the stillness. The granite cliffs border-ing the highway passed blurrily by and the colored leaves swept over the sky.

In the middle seat, John, Hope, Sarah, and Elizabeth Ruth stared out the windows waiting for someone to say something. With fingers poked in his ears sticking out around his crew cut, Ham grinned as he slowly mouthed "monkey face" at anyone who'd look, but no one did, except me and Luke in the way back with him. They started making faces at Dad hunched over the wheel. Ham pressed the silver dollar Dad had just given him into his eye so it fit perfectly, without holding it, in the socket and then he flattened his nose with it. I stopped looking. I didn't want to lose.

"I'll give you my silver dollar if you ask Dad if he dyed his hair white," Ham whispered to Luke. It was true, over the past year, Dad's hair had turned mostly white with a few drops of black, like a little paint spilled on the back of his head.

"You lost," Luke whispered back.

Hope cleared her throat loudly so they'd know she heard them talking, too.

"So did you," Ham whispered back. "Go ahead, ask him. Chicken."

"I'm not a chicken."

"Then ask him."

Luke cleared his throat and, smiling, asked, "Um, Dad, did you dye your hair white?"

Mum's gaze went from Luke to Dad and back and then her laughter started choking out of her. We all started laughing and couldn't stop.

Then Dad swerved the Oldsmobile across the middle lanes. The cars he cut off beeped back at us but sped past as we stopped in the emergency lane. No one was laughing then, and the engine went *clink, clink*. From where my head hit the seat in front of me, I could see Sarah holding the door handle with one hand, the other covering her face.

In the time it took Dad to swing himself out of the car and around the back, where he flung open the door, we had frozen in our places and were waiting for what we knew was going to happen. Before it started, we had covered our ears. The cars sped by and someone beeped and still the thwacking sounds of Dad walloping Luke over his knee right there on the side of the road came through.

Dad swung around and, pointing his finger at all of us, spat, "That's enough funny stuff. Do you hear me? I don't want to hear another word until we get to Blue Hills." It was like we were playing Dad's new silent game, where everyone lost.

Ham slid the silver dollar across the carpet to Luke, but he wouldn't look at Ham or the coin.

The way home was different, though. That's the way it always is — bad luck, then good luck. You never know which comes first. We ate McIntosh apples and salted peanuts out of their shells.

"You should have seen your face when you were holding that boa constrictor during the snake show," Hope said to Ham.

"Yeah, everyone thought you were going to faint," Luke said, spitting up his chewed apple.

"I wasn't scared. That snake must have weighed about a thousand pounds!" Ham shouted.

"Why'd you say you'd do it if you were too weak to hold it?" John asked.

"He wasn't scared," I yelled. "Besides, Elizabeth Ruth is too scared to touch that snake under the blue stones."

"I am not!" Elizabeth Ruth screamed. "I just never felt like it. They're slimy."

"Shhh, shhh," Dad said.

John howled. "That's a good one."

"I bet no one else would have held a boa," Ham said to me.

"Yeah, sure," Luke cried out. "If I were an animal, I'd be a lion. I'd rip that snake to pieces.

"What?" he asked when we laughed. "I would."

"If I were an animal, I'd be a giraffe," Elizabeth Ruth said, stretching her head forward.

"A giraffe? Who would want to be a giraffe?"

"Elizabeth Ruth, so she can stick her nose everywhere she can't reach now," Hope said.

"What would you be, Dad?" Sarah asked.

"A gorilla," Ham whispered.

"He already is one," I said into his ear.

"I'd be an otter," he answered. "They seem like they're always happy."

For a minute, no one said anything, then Ham yelled from the back, "But you can't swim, Dad!"

"Sure I can."

"Why don't you then?"

"I'd be an otter, too," Mum said. "I'd swim and eat all day long."

"I'd be a dog," Ham yelled. "I am a dog. Woof, woof." He hung his tongue out of his mouth and licked my face. He lapped my fingers.

"Good dog," I said.

"I'd be — " Hope started.

"A fat cow," John finished for her.

"I'd be a wild horse," she said.

"I'd tear your throat out," Luke said.

"Luke," Mum said.

"If Ham's a dog, then does Emily have to be a dog, too?" Sarah asked.

"Yeah, dog twins." John laughed.

"Woof, woof."

"No, I want to be a whole," I said.

"A hole?" Hope asked.

"I mean, I don't want to be a dog twin. Not a half," I started to say.

"Can't we get a dog, Dad?" Ham asked.

"No, no pets," he answered.

"Why, Dad? Why?"

"Yeah, why, Dad?"

"It's too much work for your mother."

"Can we please get a dog, Mum?"

"You have to ask your father."

"Can we, Dad?"

"No."

"Why not?"

"Because I said so, that's why." He spun his head around to glare at us.

"What would you be, Sarah?" Mum asked.

"A bird," she said quietly. Behind us the sun was an orange sinking down.

"She'd be a free bird." Hope laughed.

"Cuz I'm as free as a bird," someone sang.

"He's coming, shut the door," Sarah says now, slamming her door.

I open my eyes and see the bright blue sky above me. I wish I were a bird now. I'd fly out of this Oldsmobile the sun is beating through, keeping us hot and cramped. I'd fly away home instead of waiting another second for Dad.

Dad pokes his smiling red face into the car. "Hi, kids, ready to go?"

"Yes, Dad."

He draws on a pink paper umbrella stuck in his mouth like a cigar and laughs, wanting us to laugh with him. He revs the engine, then jets forward as we suck air, trying to catch ourselves. My stomach turns. I grab onto the seat. My head lifts to the sky.

"Jack's mother-in-law broke her hip," he tells us. Dad can't stop laughing. He's almost choking. "Fell down the stairs. So I said to him, 'Jack, what'd you do, push her down?' And he goes, 'No, I kicked her.'" Dad shakes his head and laughs some more, his face shining, his hair blowing back, and his thick hands gripping the steering wheel. Back on 128, the pavement is disappearing beneath us, becoming smaller and smaller as we get bigger, faster and bigger, until I think my head's going to snap.

"'No, I kicked her,'" he says.

I press my face into my nylon bathing suit, inhaling its clean plasticy smell. I won't wear it. Never. I spread my hands over the seat cover, slipping one into the crease of the seat, hot and filled with sand and peanut shells. I scoop them up into my fist, then spread them out flat to blow the shells, making the same wish I always make.

When we pull into the driveway, he slams on the brakes and jumps out, leaving his door open. "London bridge is falling down, falling down, falling down," Hope sings.

Elizabeth Ruth and I squat down to measure Dad's skid marks in the dirt beneath the stones. Each one is a little less than the length from my shoulder to the top of my middle finger. "Not as long as the last time," Elizabeth Ruth says, smiling.

I spot a turtle by the exhaust pipe, making its way toward me. It has a beaked nose, a scalloped shell, and a pointed tail. Right away I name him Birdy. No one is looking out from the kitchen window. I kick off one of my sneakers, pick him up, and drop him in there, tilting my shoe so he slides down into the toe. *Stay, Birdy, stay,* I tell him. I have something of my own. Birdy scuttles along the worn inner part of my sneaker, then slides backward into the toe again. The sound makes my heart beat faster.

"London bridge is falling down." Elizabeth Ruth echoes Hope, making a half bridge by lifting her arms in an arch. Hope places her palms flat against Elizabeth Ruth's, connecting the bridge for Sarah, me, and Birdy to go under. I better hide him. I better keep him safe, I say to myself and run with my sneaker inside my shirt, through London bridge before it falls down.

As soon as I have Birdy in a shoe box, I hear Dad calling everybody to help wash the Oldsmobile.

Hope is already hosing the top of the car, gleaming like a bald spot in the sun. I wash the whitewalls until they're so white, I'm sure they'll catch Dad's eye. I scrub around and around the ring with my S.O.S. scouring pad until the gray lather sits there in a perfect circle. Then I look over at Hope so she'll know it's time to hose off my tire. When she finally sees me waiting for her, she marches over with the hose bent at the neck.

"Do you think I'm a mind reader?" she asks, standing above me. "I'm supposed to get the sound waves from your galaxy to earth? Well, I hate to tell you, but I'm only human — unlike you. Watch out."

Hope shoots the water into the pebbles of the driveway so it wells into a puddle around my sneakers. She keeps it there, spraying across my legs. Elizabeth Ruth sets her soapy dishrag up on the hood of the car to watch, as Hope presses her thumb over the stream of water and sprays me. It hurts when the water hits my ankles, my knees, my thighs, the tops of my thighs, my private. So I hold myself around the knees.

"Why don't you tell me to stop it?" she shrieks. "Why don't you say *something*? Or are you from outer space?"

"Leave her alone, Hope." Sarah knots up the green, yellow-striped hose so it will stop spraying me. In the glare of the sun, Sarah's eyes are the brightest blue — just like Ham's. She says, "You think you're so great."

"You think you're so great." Hope sticks her bossy face in the air.

From around the corner Dad suddenly comes, carrying a weathervane with a rusted whale at the end. "Where are your brothers?" he calls out to us.

"Am I my brothers' keeper?" Hope says back too loudly.

Dad drops the weathervane to the ground and walks over fast to rip the hose out of Hope's grip. The hose slips out of Sarah's hands, too, and the water unbuckles furiously, squirting him all at once. In a few seconds Dad is dripping, from his hair down to his scowling face, over his short-sleeved button-down, until he tightens the hose into another messy knot. Hope half-laughs.

"Shut off the goddamn stupid hose, somebody," he shouts as he begins looping the slack hose in circles around his elbow. Now the water is stopping, then spurting slowly.

"Do you still think it's funny?" he asks Hope, lashing the few extra yards of hose out at her.

Hope blocks her face as Dad lashes the hose at her. The metal nozzle makes a cracking sound when it hits her finger or her head, I can't tell which. It all happens so fast. The hose coils around her, then uncoils. She ducks, hiding her face from Dad. He is like a snake pitcher pitching the snake to Hope. His eyes are yellow slits and his angry mouth a forked tongue as he plants his feet, throwing the snake at Hope.

Then it begins to stop. The snake coils into neat loops and falls asleep, disappearing back into the garden hose. The hose spurts a little, hisses and strikes, then is quiet at last. I untuck my spinning head to see Bud staring over at us from behind the rhododendrons. He barks sharply at us.

I am my brother's keeper.

4

No one wants to go over to the new neighbors' house to welcome them with Mum's homemade raisin bread. "You should be thankful you have the arms and legs to do it at all," Mum says and sends me and Elizabeth Ruth over.

"Hi," the man says, holding his front door open with his toe and then letting it shut to keep the black cat wrapping around his leg from escaping through the door. I see speckles of dust and paint in his wavy brown hair.

"Hi," Elizabeth Ruth says.

I wave, standing behind Elizabeth Ruth, who explains, "That's my sister Emily. She doesn't talk."

"Oh," he says, shifting his weight onto his other leg. He's wearing old jeans and a ripped T-shirt also splattered with paint. His face is tan, which makes his teeth look too white when he grins at Elizabeth Ruth. "But you do."

"I'm Elizabeth Ruth." She stands with one hand on her hip and the other hand pushing the plastic-wrapped raisin bread toward him. "My mother made this for you."

"I'm Ray. Come on in, if you want. I'm fixing the place up." She steps right in. "Oh, and this is Sticks." He sweeps the black cat up in his free arm. I watch them through the screen.

"Are you a carpenter?" she asks.

"Of sorts, yeah," he answers. "I'm living here for a while, fixing it up for a friend. I needed a place to stay and he needed someone to fix the place up. Where do you live?"

"Right at the end of the road." She points in the direction of our house, tilting her head to the side, the corners of her lips pulling up.

"The house with all the kids?" he asks. "There was an old woman who lived in a shoe. She had so many children —"

"I've heard that one before," Elizabeth Ruth says.

"Why doesn't your sister talk?" he asks.

"Just doesn't." She shrugs.

"Well, have a look around."

With my forehead pressed to the screen door, I follow Ray around the cardboard boxes, cans of paint, drop cloths, ripped-up carpet, frilly shades, and old books piled in the center of the room. The walls are bare except for drop cloths lining the baseboards. Ray's too skinny, I decide, watching him open the refrigerator door and pull out a beer. He leans his skinny hip against the kitchen counter and tilts his long arm back to drink his beer. "Well, tell your mother thanks a lot for the bread. I can't remember the last time I had homemade bread."

"Doesn't your wife cook?"

"I just got divorced," he says, "but my wife definitely didn't cook, unless you count that frozen crap. And she always burned that."

I lift my face from the screen. Wait until Dad hears about this. When I look again, Elizabeth Ruth is taking a sip of his beer.

"How old are you, Elizabeth?"

"Sixteen," she lies. "Almost."

He smiles. "Want to see the rest of the house?"

She follows him upstairs.

On the way home, Elizabeth Ruth is practically singing when she tells me, "I've got to get this beer taste out of my mouth." She giggles. "He said I could come back any time I wanted. He's so cute. What if he's over thirty? I'm not going to tell *anyone*."

I squeeze my arm to make sure I'm anyone.

"What are they like?" Mum asks, glancing up from the bread board, where she is slicing tomatoes.

"Nice, really nice."

"It's such a small house. Do they have any children?"

"No." Elizabeth Ruth giggles.

"What's so funny? I can't wait to tell Mrs. Riley. She'll want to know everything. What's he do?"

"Construction stuff. He's fixing up the house."

"Oh, nice. What's she like?"

"Small with black hair and a little white under her chin." Elizabeth Ruth laughs. "*She's* a cat. He's *divorced* from his wife."

"Oh my heavens, how long's he staying, I wonder. Better not say anything," she says. She quickly adds, "Go wash your hands."

Elizabeth Ruth runs upstairs, and I drag the bench over to the kitchen sink.

"Just what we need," Mum continues, shaking her head. "Especially if he finds out I sent up some raisin bread." She turns her head to me as if she suddenly realizes I'm there. "Well, at least I know you won't say anything." She laughs. The baby starts crying from his crib in the living room. "Go rock him, would you please, Emily."

Dad finds out that night. His eyes are blue ice as he bellows across the supper table, staring out over us, freezing us. "I'll tell you why the divorce rate is so high. They're a bunch of degenerates. They think they can sit around all day with that long hair, take drugs, have premarital sex, and do whatever else they want to do. There are no values, no beliefs, no respect. It's a goddamn shame."

We listen, eating our grilled cheese sandwiches.

"This guy Ray, he's a real winner. He was laying in the middle of his lawn when I drove by. I thought something happened to the guy, but he said he was looking at the sky. 'Peace,' that's what he said. Peace my ass. He was probably high on marijuana. I don't want anyone near his house, do you hear me?"

"Yes, Dad." We nod and watch him get up to fix a tall glass of whiskey and ginger ale to drink in his office with a couple slices of white bread. We wait for the familiar click of the TV, the TV voice, then the door to shut.

"Who's this?" Hope jumps up and asks us. Hunching her shoulders and staring out into space, she shuffles along the kitchen floor like Dad, carrying a pretend glass in her hand. "They're all degenerates, unlike me. I just drink all day long," she says in Dad's low voice. I laugh with them even though I see Dad's face in her face.

We all start laughing. Even Mum is smiling as she says, "Stop it, Hope. That's terrible."

"It's got to be that long hair they have."

"Guess that makes us all pagans," Sarah says.

"Not me." Elizabeth Ruth tosses her short hair.

"You're more of a pagan than any of us," Hope tells her.
"What about Ernie?" Luke asks.

"Ernie's crazy, isn't he, Mum?" Elizabeth Ruth adds.

"Of course not," Mum answers. "He's, well, a bit eccentric."

"Eccentric people live in New York. They have poodles and stuff, they don't get arrested," Hope says.

"That's enough, Hope." Mum sighs as Dad's office door opens.

*   *   *

It's a good thing Dad doesn't know anything about Elizabeth Ruth going over Ray's the very next day. She waits until Dad comes in from the garage to go to the bathroom and get a snack and another cup of coffee. Then as soon as he goes back to the garage, Elizabeth Ruth sneaks away, running through the woods to Ray's, two houses up on the right. Even though the Coopers are in Florida, Elizabeth Ruth still cuts through the woods, behind the Coopers' house to the blackberry bushes running wild along Ray's backyard.

She doesn't see me crouch down behind the blackberry bushes to watch her watching Ray scraping paint and singing to the radio blasting through the kitchen window. At first Ray doesn't notice her, so she strolls around the deck, finally stretching herself out on the green-and-white-striped lawn chair. Peels of white paint fall onto the drop cloth draped over the bushes below as he scrapes above her. When he starts climbing down the ladder, he finally waves and calls, "Hi, Liz."

She doesn't tell him that she hates being called Liz. She stretches out her leg, pointing her toe, twirling it in the air. She sings along to the song playing on the radio.

"I've been working my ass off," he says, wiping the sweat from his forehead. "What kind of music do you like, Liz?"

"The Rolling Stones and the Beatles. What about you?"

"You know, Zeppelin and Skynyrd and stuff," he says, examining his hands. "Hey, would you mind getting me a cold beer? My hands are a mess."

"Sure." She jumps up.

When she comes back out, he's sitting on half of her chair with his legs swung to the side. She cracks the beer open and hands it to him. "Need anything else?"

"I bet you make a great tuna sandwich," he says, smiling.

"I do." Elizabeth Ruth's face lights up.

"Everything's on the counter." He leans back in the chair, taking long sips of his beer.

A few minutes later she's carrying the sandwich on a plate in front of her.

"Wow, this looks great. You are something else." He takes off his shirt and spreads his legs on either side of the chair, setting the plate on his lap. "Would you mind just grabbing me another can of beer? And have whatever you want. There's a box of Oreos in there."

This time when she comes back, he takes the cold can of beer and tips it in the air toward her. Before he cracks it open, he presses it against the side of her bare leg. "Cold, huh?"

He drags his eyes up and down her. "I bet you have a lot of boyfriends in school, Liz."

"My dad doesn't really let us date."

"That's not very nice of him."

Elizabeth Ruth twists the end of her T-shirt into a tight ball, tucks it under itself to show off her belly button. "Can I open these?" she asks, holding up the box of Oreos.

"You can eat them all if you want."

Elizabeth Ruth sits cross-legged beside him on the porch. Everything seems to be in slow motion in the hazy summer heat. The bees buzz in circles around the blackberries starting to turn purple. I can feel the hot boards on her legs as she sits there twisting off one side of the Oreo, licking the frosting, nibbling around the edges of one wafer, then the other. Mum never buys Oreos. Sometimes she lets us put them in the wagon with Scooter Pies, colored ice cream cones, and Froot Loops cereal. She lets us keep them in the wagon until we get to the register, then someone, usually Hope, has to go return them all while the rest of us help with the bagging.

I want to be Elizabeth Ruth licking the insides of the Oreos and popping them into her mouth. Leaning back, she shakes her head in the sun. She is smiling funny at him. They stare at each other. I feel funny. Something inside of me tickles. When he opens his mouth, Elizabeth Ruth puts an Oreo between his lips. She pulls her hand back, laughing. She looks so happy. Heat rushes up the sides of my face, making my hot head spin around and around. I know we are doing something wrong, Elizabeth Ruth and I.

When the echo of Mum calling, "Youu-whoo," reaches us, paralyzing me, I let that feeling of walking out of a dark movie theater into sharp daylight wash over me. Elizabeth Ruth walks inside with the Oreos and the empty plate. I want to stay here in Ray's backyard and find out what happens, but instead I run through the beams of light shining between the trees in the back-woods, all the way home.

Hope wants to know where we've been when we arrive separately, Elizabeth Ruth seconds after me, both of us out of breath. Elizabeth Ruth shrugs, answering, "Woods."

We eat cucumber sandwiches on Mum's oatmeal bread while Mum spoons mashed potato into the baby's mouth. Mum is worried because he's been fussing all morning and might have an ear infection. She doesn't ask why Elizabeth Ruth and I were late, or why Elizabeth Ruth isn't eating anything. She doesn't say anything except, "Tchh, tchh, tchh." As soon as the dishes are cleared, she tells us, "Everyone outside until suppertime."

"Mum, it's about a thousand degrees out," Luke complains.

"You're lucky you can go outside and play at all. Some poor children have to sit in a hospital bed all day."

"I wish I could sit in bed all day," Luke says.

"Don't talk like that, Luke. How would you like to be all crippled?"

We go back to the muddy part of the river to jump from

stump to stump all the way to the other end of yard and the wild bramble runs along the edge of the garden. Luke wanders through the mess of overgrown woods as if he's trying to find something. John's working at the bike shop in town. We travel around the world in the swamp.

"I'm the Queen of Spain," Hope says. She spreads her legs as far as her jean skirt will let her, one leg on each stump, one hand keeping her balance, and the other pulling her underwear to the side. She pees straight and forceful, watching it jet into the swampy water, bubbling up. "Look, I'm peeing standing up," she calls back to Sarah. "Did you hear me?

"I'm going to teach all of you to piss standing up. That'll be the beginning. You'll see," Hope tells us, with her hands on her hips and her hair swinging along her back.

Elizabeth Ruth and I jump over to Sarah's west coast. "Why would we want to piss like a racehorse?" Elizabeth Ruth asks Hope. Hope jumps toward us.

"Off my California!" Sarah warns.

"It's a free country," Hope yells back.

"If it's a free country, then why do we have to go back to Martha's Vineyard?" Sarah asks.

Hope stops. We all stop and stare at her, waiting for an answer. The bees are buzzing so loud in the bramble they feel like they're inside my ear.

"I don't know," Hope finally answers. "But I have a good idea. I think we should all meet secretly. Like our own society."

"A secret society?" Elizabeth Ruth asks.

"Yeah, of pagans." She laughs, flipping her long hair back. "Let's meet out here tonight. We'll make our own rules, and one thing's for sure, we won't have any crazy people. Just us four. After supper by the clothesline."

Birdy is scratching my leg through my shorts pocket. I put him in here right before lunch. Maybe he's hungry, scrambling up my pocket. I have to hold my hand over him to tell him to stay. *Stay, boy, stay. Good boy.*

That's what I'd say to Ham when he was a dog on his hands and knees, barking. *Stay, boy.* He'd curl up at my feel, growling if anyone came near. *Good boy.* He'd lap my face.

"Dogs don't go to school," he'd say to Mum. "Woof, woof."

"Smart dogs do. Now get up and eat your breakfast, doggie."

Once in a while on a Saturday, Mum would let him eat his cereal in a bowl on the floor in our room.

After school, we'd run through the woods, trotting, sniffing the leaves, under logs, barking, sending the birds up into the treetops. "Lie down," I'd tell him and he would. I'd lie down, too, like him, only the sky between us.

My leg tickles. *Stay, Birdy,* I say, pushing him down into my pocket. When I look down I see a group of ants carrying a bee, a leg between each pair of pincers, over the cherry tree's velvety petals beside me. On the other side of me, along a crooked root lifted out of the dirt, an earth-colored spider runs clockwise, then counterclockwise, showering an invisible web over everything.

After supper, as soon as it gets dark, we go around back to the clothesline. Elizabeth Ruth brings brown paper bags from Star Savers for us to sit on. "We'll learn to do everything that men can do. Like peeing standing up, like I showed you," Hope begins, walking in circles around us. She stops in front of Elizabeth Ruth. "Elizabeth Ruth, I know you've been sneaking off. I don't know where you've been, but we can't keep secrets from each other. We need to know everything. We need to know what everyone's doing." Tapping her foot, Hope waits for Elizabeth Ruth to say something.

"I went over to check the blackberries, but they weren't ripe."

"They're never ripe this early. You know that." Hope sneers. The mosquitoes are buzzing. "Have you been talking to the divorced man?"

"Not really."

"What's that mean, Elizabeth Ruth?"

She confesses, "He lets me sit on his back porch. That's all."

Sarah gasps. "Dad would kill you if he found out."

Hope turns to Sarah. "Well, you aren't eating anything at dinner. You're always running your fork through your meat loaf or mashed potatoes or whatever else, spreading them across your plate, but you never eat anything."

Hope's right. All Sarah eats are saltines and rolled up balls of Star white bread. She takes the crust off, then tears a slice into quarters or sixths and pinches each section together one at a time, then pops them into her mouth.

"We have to start watching out for each other. He's not going to tell us what to do all the time." Hope squats down in our circle. Slowly she is pulling us into the bright blue of her eyes. For a moment the picture of us on her eyeball contains the whole world, but when Dad's voice cuts through us, she blinks and it all disappears.

"Hey, what's going on out there?" Dad yells from where he is standing next to last winter's log pile. "Better watch out for the big bad wolf. Ahhhh-woooo." Cupping his big hands on either side of his mouth, he howls; his laughter rises and echoes over the treetops, over the baby's crying, making the logs shake up and down in the woodpile. None of us budges.

"Time for bed," he calls out, then walks back inside the house.

"Is he going insane, or what?" Hope grumbles.

"Bluebells, bluebells, eevy, ivey overhead, Daddy's in the parlor cutting off his head. Chop, chop, chop," Elizabeth Ruth sings.

"We better go." Sarah starts to get up.

"Wait a minute, first we have to do something," Hope says. She twitches and smiles, then her eyes get that cold glow that means she is planning to do something cruel. "I'm thinking of a number between one and ten. Whoever is furthest from my number has to go into the garage right now and take something of his. And you have to say your number out loud."

I feel the number in my mouth, a two curling out along my tongue. I open my mouth, I want to say it. The *t* sound is on the edge of my teeth, but I can't make it come out.

"Five," Sarah blurts out.

"Nine," Elizabeth Ruth follows.

"Emily?"

The darkness swallows me.

"Okay, if you're not going to say a number, then go ahead," Hope says, crossing her arms, laughing at me. Her eyes are like Dad's. "And don't forget to bring something back."

I start walking fast — half to get away from her and half because I have to. I can't even feel myself until Birdy's sharp claw presses into my shorts leg. In the dark, it feels like someone is following me. I open the sliding glass door on the side of the garage and step into his clutter of things looming all around me. I focus on a box marked "Florida Navel Oranges" with the words "Don't Touch" written in black marker beneath it. There are long rolls of thin tracing paper next to the box and around it I see paintbrushes, wrenches, hammers, screwdrivers, cut milk cartons of eight-, nine-, and tenpenny nails, rolled up hoses, the old lawn mower. There are pieces of loose piping, handsaws, cans of turpentine, Windex, WD-40, paintbrushes, pieces of two-by-fours, drills, tubs, sand, tubs marked with numbers for different rose seeds, wrenches, Maxwell House tins full of stems, powders, chemicals, chain oil, lanterns, sawdust and dust covering everything.

Around the butcher-block, plastic tubs of Tiger Soap are set up on the pine shelves; pieces of lanterns, boxes of old inventions sit on a plank between two sawhorses; chicken feathers and feather dust cover the trash barrels; small red and green Schwinn bikes lay next to the wagon whose handle is tied with a rope and whose bed holds the five-gallon container of gasoline. I see Dad's fishing pole sticking out through the trapdoor at the top of the attic stairs. The reel dangles from the pole broken in two, the line hanging down like a spider's web, a rubber eel still hooked on the end. The shadows move behind me and I am sure someone is watching me. I hold my hand over Birdy inside my pocket so he can't escape. A madness, a humming, a buzzing sound grows louder, surrounding me like water. My ears fill with the echo of ocean waves, rising and falling.

Dad's face was twisted rubber like in the cartoons when someone gets punched or knocked so hard his face stays stuck in the place it was hit. Ham's face was floating in the sea. I had to get out. The current took us both. I was choking on the seawater, I couldn't breathe.

The first thing I saw on the shore on the other side of the bridge was a flounder or a bass tossed to the side, its cut head hanging over the edge of the rock. A fisherman had left its ripped-out insides, fluorescent white in the sun. There was a pile of seven or eight gutted fish lying on top of one another at the edge of the water. Their silver-gray faces poked into life with each jab from the seagulls picking out the last bits of bloody insides. The gulls took turns pecking, digging closer to the head of the fish, then stopped to clean their bills, dipping, fluffing up the seawater, swinging their bills in the air. I threw up all over the rocks. I threw up everything inside of me.

On the other jetty, Dad howled a sound I never heard before. The man who had pulled Ham out of the water was kneeling beside him, his clothes dripping wet, beside Dad, pumping Ham's chest with fists, blowing air into his bleeding mouth, howling into Ham. Dad's clothes were still dry.

The biggest seagull flaunted its dark wings, chasing the others away. A crow started yanking the whole top piece of rubbery loose skin from the underneath part of the dead fish.

Dad threw himself on the rocks. Then the man in the wet clothes helped us into the car, me in the front and Dad and Ham in the back. Ham's skin was blue, his mouth red. Before Dad told me to turn around in my seat, I saw red come pouring out of the hole under Ham's chin.

"Talk to me, please say something, William."

But Ham didn't say anything. He couldn't talk.

"Hold your head up, that's it," Dad said. "That's a boy."

The blood spilled on Dad's lap. I couldn't get close enough.

Everywhere I look I see red. Someone's eyes are peering through me. I take one last look around, grab a tub of Tiger Soap, and run out of the garage.

Today when I check Mum's calendar, I realize it is August 3, Sarah's and Nana's birthday. But that's not why today is different from every other day. Today I belong to something, I'm a member of something. Yesterday I was nothing.

Before I find the Tiger Soap I left in a clump of mustard swamp flowers last night, I watch to see where Dad is going after he cleans the chicken coop. He has pulled out each of the wooden bottoms of the hens' nests like drawers and is pouring steaming water over them. Then he sweeps the cement floor, sprinkling fresh sand over it, and fills the water vessel half full.

Shaking his head, he looks up at the clear sky and murmurs, "Idiot games." Taking a deep breath with his hands on his hips, he puffs himself up and says it louder, "Idiot games."

I don't know what Dad means and think he might be talking to me because, when he sees me watching him, he squints, his face tightening. He looks around and calls Bud, who comes running between us to Dad's outstretched hand.

"Good dog, thatta boy." When he looks up at me again, he seems surprised that I'm still here. He says, "Isn't it almost time to go to your grandmother's, Emily?"

I leave him there, patting Bud.

As soon as I'm in the car with everyone except Dad and John, I close my eyes and keep them closed until we are back on 128 going south. Mum's driving in the slow lane with the speedometer at forty miles per hour. It usually takes an hour to drive to Hull, but at this speed, it'll take all day, and I'm hungry. I wish I could ask Mum for a sandwich from the picnic basket. I wish I could say that and that's all, but I can't. I'm afraid I'll say everything.

Luke is in the way back, holding a Gerber baby food jar with two grasshoppers inside. "Why do I always have to sit in the back?" he complains. "Why can't Elizabeth Ruth sit back here for once?"

"Do we *have* to go?" Elizabeth Ruth whines.

"Sometimes you have to do things you don't want to," Mum says. The only good thing about going to Nana's is taking the wet naps, ketchup and mayonnaise packets, lobster bibs, books of matches, samples of shampoo or hand lotion, and other free restaurant and hotel things stuffed in all her kitchen drawers and cabinets.

Sweat is making my legs stick to the car seat. Luke unscrews the jar lid poked with holes and the two green specks are taken by the wind through the window into the open blue highway air.

"I wish I didn't have any arms or legs today so I didn't have to visit Nana and dumb Blackie," Elizabeth Ruth says back to Mum.

"Don't say that, Elizabeth Ruth."

Hope is smiling into the front mirror, showing her teeth, then closing her mouth. "Is it true the devil is a big black dog on a chain?" she asks, her teeth showing.

"It is," Mum answers. "If you don't get too close, he'll leave you alone."

"What if I go too close by accident?" she asks.

"You won't."

"Blackie's the devil, then?" Hope pinches her full lips together.

"Blackie's just a big poodle." Mum grips the steering wheel. We're going seventy miles per hour. My arms and legs are shaking from the vibration of the Oldsmobile. I have to grip the car seat on either side of me to hold steady.

I turn from Hope in the front seat to Luke, checking behind him, through the open window where the grasshoppers disappeared.

"What are you staring at?" he asks. "What's wrong with you, Emily?"

I keep thinking of the way Dad looked at me outside the chicken coop, wondering what I did. I wonder why Dad is always looking at me like that — cold and suspicious — like he did this morning. Like last summer when we were getting fish for supper. I came out carrying the fish wrapped in white paper to where Dad and Ham were parked with the engine running. As I was about to open the door, Dad jerked the car ahead about five yards, stopped, and yelled, leaning through his window, "Are you going to get in now?"

I ran again, and right when I touched the doorknob, Dad jerked ahead a few more yards. The next time he let me in. I was breathing so hard in the backseat, I couldn't talk. "Remember, no crybabies," Dad said, talking a gulp of his Coke before he passed the can to Ham. Ham was always Dad's favorite.

"Stop staring at me, Emily," Luke says. "Mum, Emily's staring at me."

"Emily," Mum says, "stop staring. It's not nice manners."

"Maybe she got too close to the big black dog," Elizabeth Ruth says.

"Emily," Sarah says, putting her hand on my shoulder. The touch of her fingers goes right to the core of me. "Are you okay?"

Mum looks at me through the rearview mirror.

I nod.

The flabby pouches under Mum's upper arms are jiggling side to side as she leans into her seat, sighing. "I can't believe how old and fat I'm getting. Sometimes I look into the mirror and ask myself, 'Who is this person?'"

"No, you're not," Sarah tells her. Sarah keeps her hand on my shoulder. Her arm is as thin as a stick and I'm sure she's secretly hoping she'll never have flab that shakes like Mum's.

When we get to Nana's, I stay in the Oldsmobile while Mum rings the doorbell for at least ten minutes. Sarah stands on the tips of her toes, peeking into the garage where Nana stores her potter's wheel and all her molds of fancy poodles, ladies with parasols, Santa sleighs and Christmas trees. All of Dad's old science projects are in there, too, most of them with first-prize ribbons attached. My favorite one is the volcano that is erupting with cotton ball clouds and oozing gooey red lava. Nana's always tells us what a genius Dad is. He's the perfect one. According to Nana, he never did anything wrong. "Compared to Ernie, who wouldn't seem perfect?" Hope asks us.

We always ask her to show us photos of Dad when he was a boy, but she must not have any, because none of us has ever seen them. Ham was sure Dad was never little and that's why there are no photos. If we think Dad is big, Ernie is huge. I just hope Ernie doesn't decide to come home one day when we're visiting. That's all we need.

"That's strange," Mum says to us. "She knows we're coming."

"Ask the birds. The birds will know." Elizabeth Ruth mimics Nana. Elizabeth Ruth doesn't care that Nana's not here. "Let's eat, Mum," she says, tossing back her straight brown hair.

Luke searches for grasshoppers beneath the ash tree. The grass has turned a dry yellow-brown. A stone wall runs across the lawn to the side of Nana's house. Where this wall meets the house,

Blackie is barking and growling, spitting at the inside of the window.

Mum lowers the picnic basket to the ground and, sighing, takes the net, bobby pins, barrettes, and rubber bands from her bun so her hair falls loosely over her shoulders. The last time she cut her hair, she made one straight cut across the bottom inch of hair in her ponytail and was done with it. Even though it's long in the front, kind of jagged, I think it looks beautiful hanging at her shoulders.

"Emily, come out of the car and have some lunch with us," Mum calls. She spreads out the cold chicken salad sandwiches on Star Savers white bread, butter on one slice, mayonnaise and mustard on the other. I am hungry. I slide out of the hot Oldsmobile and go over to where they are.

Leaning on one elbow on the grass beneath the ash tree, Mum looks so happy with her dark hair falling to the side of her face. My head fits perfectly on the curve of her hip. She runs her hand through my hair. I watch Elizabeth Ruth chew her sandwich, her mouth moving up and down. I wonder if she could ever be like Ham was.

Blackie is pawing at the window and growling at us. He doesn't let up.

"There she is!" Luke yells out, pointing to the window next to where Blackie is finally quiet. The lace curtain sways slightly inside and Blackie is finally quiet.

I sit up. Mum sits up, tucking in the white blouse that has come out of her wraparound skirt.

"Inside?" Elizabeth Ruth asks for all of us.

"Yes, Nana's inside. I saw her," he exclaims. He runs over to stand beneath the window. "Right through here."

"Maybe she didn't hear the doorbell," Sarah says, rising.

"She heard it all right. She heard it all right," Mum says. Then she says it one more time. Clutching the window ledge, Luke hops up, trying to spy on Nana again. I have to spit out the chicken, like sawdust in my mouth.

"Why doesn't Nana like us?" Luke asks.

The hot air hisses through the dry grass. Mum packs everything up and waves us toward the Oldsmobile.

Mum brushes her hair back with her small hand and says, "I thought everything would change when we got married. I thought we'd be different." She laughs to herself, gathering her hair into a ponytail, which she then circles with a net, sticks with bobby pins, and holds in place with a barrette on either side.

"Why doesn't Nana like us?" Luke repeats.

"I don't know. If you ask me, they don't like anyone, not even each other," she answers and turns the key in the ignition.

"Why did you marry him?" Hope asks through the sound of the engine turning.

"He was so good-looking," she says.

"Dad?" Hope asks. "Yuck."

"He was," Mum answers. "But Grandma and Grandpa didn't want me to marry him."

"Why, Mum?"

"Why?"

"They just didn't, that's all." She has said enough. She looks in the mirror, rubbing her lips together. "Come on, let's go finish our picnic."

"What's inside that wooden box in the top of his closet, Mum? Did his father give it to him? Do you know?" Elizabeth Ruth asks.

Leaning closer to Mum, we all look at each other without saying a word because everyone has been through the top shelf of his closet, where he keeps his Air Force cap, the Red Sox baseball he caught and had signed by Ted Williams, an oval framed photo of him on his First Communion, the original Magic Rose, and the locked wooden box.

"How do you know about it?" Mum turns to Elizabeth Ruth.

"What's inside?" Elizabeth Ruth asks.

"I don't know. It's locked." She pauses. "He never told me."

"It doesn't make a sound when you shake it and it doesn't weigh anything," Hope says.

"Tchh, tchh, tchh," Mum says, pulling out of Nana's driveway. We drive to the end of the road, where there is a dirt parking lot overlooking the ocean, to eat the rest of the chicken salad sandwiches. Waves break on the hard sand and the seagulls swoop along the water's edge, screaming as they float down to the sand. Ask the birds, the birds will know, Nana says. They saw everything. What will they tell us?

The driveway is empty, which means Dad is out somewhere in his pickup. Of course, the first thing Elizabeth Ruth does is sneak over to Ray's house. Ray is wearing a pair of cutoff jean shorts as he slaps the brush over the clapboards, painting the triangular peak in back of the house a forest green. "Long time no see."

She says back, "You're so high up."

"Yeah, well, someone's got to get up there," Ray says, carefully stepping down the ladder, holding his paint bucket out to the side. "I was wondering if you were going to come back. I missed you, Liz."

"I had to go to my grandmother's."

"How's Grandma?"

Elizabeth Ruth shrugs.

Ray wipes the sweat off his forehead. "Whew, I could really use a beer."

"I'll get it for you." His eyes follow her inside.

Elizabeth Ruth brings out two cans of Budweiser, one for Ray and one for her. They sit on the back step, the sun beating down on them. I crouch closer to the ground in the shade of the woods. The sound of the crickets rises around us.

"I finished the right side of the house today," Ray says.

"Wow, that's great, Ray."

"Tomorrow I'm going to paint the other side, and then I'll move on to the front."

"You're really fast."

"Thanks. I have to be. Look, I still have the entire yard to clear. I'm going to cut all those trees down out front." His arm circles the air. Then he crushes his beer can with his hand and tosses it to the side. It rolls under the lawn chair.

Elizabeth Ruth marches into the kitchen for two more beers. She sits back down beside Ray on the porch and opens the beers, laughing as the second one goes *pshht*, spraying on his bare chest and spilling over the edge of the can into a puddle between them.

"I met your dad the other day," he says, brushing off his chest. "Boy, he's got a temper."

Elizabeth Ruth stops laughing.

"I was lying there minding my own business when he started asking me all these questions. I was like, what'd I do?"

"Yeah, I know. We're not supposed to go near your house, that's what he said."

"No shit." He laughs, slapping the side of his leg, taking a deep pull of his drink. "Why's he so uptight?"

Elizabeth Ruth shrugs.

"I guess it's not easy having so many kids. What's he do?"

"He's an inventor."

"No shit. What'd he invent?"

"The Magic Rose."

"Never heard of it." He pauses. "I don't know any inventors."

"I don't think you're going to know my father either."

Ray laughs. "No, I don't think I want to."

"He never lets us do anything," Elizabeth Ruth blurts out. "He just makes rule after rule."

"Well, rules were made for breaking." His eyes shift to Elizabeth Ruth. "I had a dream about you last night, you know."

"You did?" The corners of her mouth curl up.

"Yeah."

"What'd I do?"

"You really want to know?"

"Yes."

"You were lying on that chair," he says, pointing to the green-and-white-striped lawn chair, "like you were yesterday. But you didn't have any clothes on."

Elizabeth Ruth takes a long sip of her beer to hide her smile.

The telephone rings inside. Ray's voice is a whirring sound as he stands in the doorway, talking and laughing into the phone. He cracks open another beer for him and places one beside Elizabeth Ruth on the back porch. He scratches his skinny chest and keeps talking into the phone like Elizabeth Ruth isn't even there. Her face shuts down, her eyes turn to the ground, her mouth becomes a single line. She is a shadow on the back porch. I want Elizabeth Ruth to be herself again.

When Elizabeth Ruth rises, she totters, then straightens herself, brushing her hair with her hand. It feels like everything is spinning around me, too. "I have to go," she tells Ray.

He holds up his finger, mouthing to Elizabeth Ruth, "One minute, Liz."

She sighs as he goes into the kitchen.

Finally, he comes back out. "You can't go yet." His fingers trace down the front of her shirt, stopping at the top snap of her shorts. His hand slides into the top of her shorts, pushing deeper inside there. He says her name. His other hand goes around the back of her and pulls her closer, down on the deck. It all happens so fast, I can't see her. He's on top of her, pushing her legs out on either side of him, his shorts around his hips. Her legs unfold. Her shorts are wrapped around the end of her sneaker.

Something terrible is happening and I am doing nothing. I want to see if her face is there, but I can't see anything except his thin body pumping up and down on top of her. *Get up, Elizabeth Ruth. Do something.* The ground shifts beneath me, sucking me into the green-gold leaves spread beside me. Her hands fly into the air to find something to hold on to. He is hurting her. I know I shouldn't look.

Mum's hands had nothing to hold on to either. I heard a tinny cry. Everyone else must have been sleeping. I couldn't sleep that night of the funeral. Then Dad saw me. His white flesh shone in the dark. He lost his balance and fell back onto Mum. Then he was running after me, chasing me.

"Oh God, oh God, oh God, Liz," Ray yells, pushing up and down on the deck, before he collapses on her. Her hands finally touch the ground. She rolls her head to the side and I think she is going to be sick. He pants, his body slowly rising and falling.

The sky seems right above me, pushing me into the ground, too. I have stopped breathing. I might throw up. When Ray rolls off her, she quickly sits up to tug her shorts back on. Her stony face doesn't look back at him when he grins at her, pointing at a spot he missed painting green on the top triangle of the house. She lifts herself up, buttoning her shorts, and walks in a crooked line, weaving off the porch.

"You're leaving already?"

"Yeah, I'm late." She doesn't look back at him with his arms folded around his head as he lies on the porch with his fly still undone.

"Well, good-bye, Liz."

She's half-running now, but she stops to yell back at him, "It's Elizabeth Ruth." She doesn't stop until she's in the woods by a patch of thick green ferns. Taking a quick look around her, she drops her shorts to rub a handful of fern leaves between her legs. She throws the used ferns to the ground, then rubs her hands in the dirt, crumbling old leaves between her palms.

I feel like I am her with my shorts down, cleaning off my private because I've done something wrong. Something terrible has happened to us. Next time, we have to stop it, I tell myself. Next time I'll do something.

The blackbirds sing their afternoon songs in the trees above us as I follow Elizabeth Ruth's crooked shadow home.

5

Elizabeth Ruth has been in the shower so long, Mum knocks on the door. "Elizabeth Ruth, I think you must be clean by now." I should wash that feeling of Ray off my skin, too, but I have just enough time before Sarah's birthday party to wrap up my old jacks and Super Ball with some toilet paper. Then I — the person who absolutely loves donuts; chocolate, chocolate coconut, butter crunch, jelly, and who could eat them for breakfast, lunch, and dinner the rest of her life — write on her birthday card, "I owe you my donut the next time we get donuts at Lord's Department Store." I carry it and my present downstairs, where Hope and Sarah, in their new sundresses, are getting supper.

The Velveeta cheese has melted over the burgers onto the grill and is beginning to brown around the edges. Hope slides the spatula beneath one of the cheeseburgers and pushes it with her finger onto the toasted bread Sarah is buttering. "When you make the potato salad, don't use as much mayonnaise as Mum does. She drowns it —" Hope breaks off, looking at me. Slowly wiping off the hamburger fat the burgers splattered on her arm, she finishes, "The potato salad, I mean, only needs a little mayonnaise, a little mustard, salt, pepper, and whatever else. Here, Emily."

Quickly Hope hands me the cutting knife and yesterday's baked potatoes and I begin peeling off the dirty skin in long strips where it has separated from the moist white inside, cutting the meaty part into cubes.

Elizabeth Ruth comes downstairs, dressed in clean white pants and a T-shirt. Her hair is neatly combed back from her face. "Want some help?" she asks, looking down at the brown potatoes. I hand her my knife, and she immediately begins peeling off the cooked skin. Her hands are shaking.

When we are all sitting at the supper table set with the elephant tablecloth from India and all the prizes, Dad says, "Must be someone's birthday." A rectangular box sits beside his place. Everyone has one. If it's your birthday, you're supposed to give everyone a prize. Putting it close to his ear, he shakes it. "Not peanuts," he says. Then he squeezes it and says, "Hmmm, not socks. I'll use my super X-ray vision to figure out what it is, kids. Just give me a few minutes." He bites into his cheeseburger.

"It's Sarah's birthday," Mum reminds him.

"No kiddin'. How old are you, champ?" Dad asks Sarah with his mouth full.

"Fifteen," she answers.

"Well, happy birthday," he says, smiling, his whole face lit up.

Every time his face glows like that I think something good is going to happen. When Dad invents something really big again, we'll probably have enough money to buy a new house somewhere far away, without chickens, without a clothesline, and without a swamp in the backyard. If we had a nice place, Dad could stop finding things to be mad about because nothing would be out of order like it is in Cawood.

"Your father wants to name the baby Owen. What do you think?" Mum asks us.

"Owen? I like it," John says.

"Owen Stone," Hope says.

Luke turns to Hope with his mouth open and full of cheeseburger and laughs.

"Is there going to be a christening?" Sarah asks.

Mum puckers her bottom lip over her top lip, waiting for Dad to answer.

"Of course." He stops chewing.

I keep watching Elizabeth Ruth staring at Bud, who is waiting by her feet. As soon as Owen starts crying in his crib a few feet from Mum, Elizabeth Ruth drops the cheeseburger on her lap to the floor. Bud swallows it in a couple bites, licks his mouth, and looks up at her for more. She pushes him away with her foot. He thinks she's playing and jumps up on her legs, his big face slobbering as his paws scramble to grab hold of her. She screams.

"Bud!" Dad yells.

Bud runs out from underneath the table to Dad and starts licking the thick hands going around his face, jumping up on Dad's knee.

"Whoa, boy, take it easy. You know you're not supposed to be under the table," Dad tells Bud, letting him jump up on him for a few more minutes before he says, pointing, "Go, Bud. Out."

Dad pushes his chair back from the table. He gets up too fast and lets out a fart, quick and loud. Silence follows until Mum says, "Well, excuse me," as if she farted.

Hope snickers.

Luke leans toward John. "It's a good place to cut a fart and run."

"What?" Dad yells. "What'd you say, mister?"

"It's a good place to cut a fart and run," Luke says, smiling.

"Where'd you hear that?"

"Mum's book."

"Is that true?" Dad whips toward Mum.

Mum nods.

"Where is it?"

She gets her Thomas Merton book from the living room and hands it to Dad, who, shaking his head, bristles. He flips through the pages, searching for the word. "Where is it?"

"They're at the Thomas Merton library. It's the first time he's seen it. He says, 'It's a good place to cut a — ' you know."

"Thomas Merton said that?" Dad shakes his head some more. "And that is what you're reading?"

Mum nods. She loves Thomas Merton.

"Junk, that's what it is. Pure junk." With Mum's book under his arm, he turns to us. "Who's ready to go to Friendly's?"

Whether we're done eating or not, we all get up to pile into the Oldsmobile, leaving Sarah's prize boxes beside our plates and leaving Mum to do the dishes with Owen. Friendly's is the *only* place to go in Cawood at night. At the last minute, Dad calls Bud to jump in the car with us. He plunges over the middle seat into the back with Luke. Mum stands on the front doorstep, waving to us until we are halfway up the street.

Ray is standing out front, gazing at his house. He smiles, turns a step toward us in the Oldsmobile, and waves in a big arc. We stare back at him. Dad guns the car forward. No one waves back. Ray's face drops at the same time as his hand does. In the front seat next to Dad, Elizabeth Ruth folds her arms across her chest, looking straight ahead at nothing.

When we get to the top of the street, Hope pulls in her breath and whispers, "Look." It's the hunchback Mr. Kosik walking in baby steps down his driveway. We gasp, sitting up straight in our seats to stare at Mr. Kosik's big lump of a back tucked over him.

"Look at his back," Luke says.

"What do you think we're looking at?" Hope whispers sharply. "It must be a sign."

"I can't believe he's out," John says.

"How'd he get like that, Dad?" Luke asks.

Dad drives slowly by his house. He shrugs. "Ask your mother. She'll tell you."

Bud barks in the backseat.

"Okay, Bud. Relax, boy," Dad reassures him.

My face goes red and hot and my back gets all itchy as I take one last look at Mr. Kosik.

"He must be at least a hundred years old," Luke says.

"Mrs. Fern told us that when someone turns one hundred, the president sends them a letter," Luke says. "Do you think Mr. Kosik will get one, Dad?"

"What? Oh, no way. Listen to your father when he tells you that there's no way that man will get a letter. No way," Dad answers, finally turning off Willow Street.

When he stops at the first traffic light, Dad asks Elizabeth Ruth, "Who's the strongest one you know?"

"You," she answers.

"Look at this. Tough as nails." At the stop sign, he flexes his right arm tight into a lump of muscle, clenching his fist and squinting. He's wearing a short-sleeved plaid button-down tucked into his work chinos. Even though his hair has turned white and there are yellow creases around his bright blue eyes when he turns and smiles at Elizabeth Ruth, he doesn't look old. "Strongest man on the planet," he tells her.

"What about Superman?" Luke shouts out from the back.

"Super weakling compared to me," Dad tells him.

"Yeah, well, look at this." Luke grunts, squeezing his arm.

"Excuse me, look at what?" Hope asks him.

"Looks like a crappy little muscle to me," John says.

"What about Ernie?" Luke blurts out. "He's stronger than you."

Now I remember. At the funeral, Ernie wore a dark wool suit that was too short in the arms and tight across the back and around the thighs. You could see his white socks. He arrived right after the mass, came in through the side, up to the altar, tipped his hat, then walked down the center aisle. He grabbed Dad from behind in a bear hug.

Something happened. Dad broke. He collapsed and fell to the ground in a broken heap. A few ladies in bright dresses screamed, threw up their hands, and came running around Dad, who just lay there on the ground. Ernie, who was taller than them all, stood back and laughed. Everyone in the church went quiet, the organist stopped playing, and the ladies in the bright dresses stepped back, horrified. I couldn't find Mum anywhere.

"Who's the strongest one, Sarah?"

"You, Dad."

"Okay, then."

The sun is going down like a red spider spreading its legs across the sky. The fresh-cut grass, barbecue, and summer air smells are coming through the window. Dad clicks on the radio to a wailing horn sound and starts strumming his thumb to the beat.

"If you really have X-ray eyes, Dad, how many fingers do I have up?" Luke calls from the back. Dad doesn't answer.

As we're about to turn into Friendly's, Bubble Gum Bill, on his bike, starts waving and ringing his bell at us, until he realizes it's not Mum driving the Oldsmobile. "Oh great," Hope says. "They let him out again. And you know he doesn't *work* at the Cawood State Hospital. He *lives* there."

"Whoa, Bill," Dad says, holding his big hand in a stop sign out his window. Bill stops in front of the car.

"Your boyfriend's here," Hope whispers over the seat to Elizabeth Ruth. "Aren't you kind of hot? Why are you wearing long pants?"

Elizabeth Ruth doesn't answer, and if there's one thing about Elizabeth Ruth, it's that she's never quiet.

"What's the matter with her?" Hope asks.

"Maybe she's sick," Sarah says.

"Who's sick?" Dad asks. "Elizabeth Ruth, are you sick?"

She shakes her head.

"You wouldn't lie to your father, would you, Elizabeth Ruth?"

"No, Dad."

I keep seeing Ray on top of her.

"Hey, Bill, you been recruited to the Red Sox?" Dad asks Bill, who is wearing a Red Sox cap and jersey.

"No, sir."

A pocket radio is strapped to the handlebars next to a walkie-talkie and attached on either side on the back of the bicycle are baskets filled with baseball cards, gum, brown bags, and a bicycle pump. Around his waist Bill wears a carpenter's belt stocked with gum, a flashlight, a pocket camera, and pens, and hanging on a leather strap around his neck is a huge ring with at least two dozen keys. When he pushes his open pack of Big Red across Dad, closer to Elizabeth Ruth, his mood ring shines bright black. She takes a piece of his gum. Hope whistles behind Elizabeth Ruth. Oh, great, I think, it's going to happen again with Bill.

"How about having an ice cream at Friendly's with the kids?" Dad asks.

"Yeah, sure," he says nervously. "Okay, okay. I just have to get some more gum at the store." Straddling the bar of his three-speed, Bill lifts the bike and duckwalks backwards, then pedals off.

Dad starts whistling to the radio again, smiling when he pulls the car into the Friendly's parking lot. At least we don't have to worry about kids from school seeing us. Hardly anyone from St. Mary's lives in Cawood.

"Okay, let's go, guys." Dad shakes his finger at Bud. "You stay. Hear me?" Dad checks the inside of his wallet and then we follow him through the doors.

John and Luke sit in a short booth across from us. Luke starts naming all the flavors he's tried from the forty-nine flavors listed on the rotating box above us. The rest of us fit in the long booth, Hope, Sarah, and me on one side and Dad and Elizabeth Ruth on the other. I watch Elizabeth Ruth chewing her Big Red and studying the Friendly's menu marked with diagrams of the Jim Dandy, the Friendly Banana Split, the Friendly Fribble, a new line of glowing sherbet coolers, and all sizes of cups and cones.

In a blue dress with a ruffled collar, our waitress pulls out her check pad from her apron pocket and begins writing as she introduces herself, blinking. "How's everybody doing tonight? I'm Caroline, I'll be your waitress. Are you ready to order?" Caroline chews her gum so it snaps through the front of her teeth, then disappears, then snaps again. She pauses to glance over her check pad at us. Like Elizabeth Ruth, she stands with one hip thrown out to the side.

"Root beer floats for everyone," Dad orders, then leans back against the cushioned red seat of the booth with one perfectly creased pant leg sticking out in the aisle, making his polished work boot look huge on the tiled floor. The last two times he bought work boots, he had to get a half size bigger. Mum says he's the only full-grown man she knows whose feet keep growing.

"Here he comes." Sarah nudges Hope.

"Try to control yourself, Elizabeth Ruth," Hope says.

"Look at how bowlegged he is. A train could run between

those legs of his," Sarah whispers back. "We should call him Cowboy Bill."

"Is that what you call him, Elizabeth Ruth?"

She pretends not to hear them.

I try to remember what Ray's legs look like and wonder if they're bowlegged or not.

Standing there grinning so we can see all the yellow teeth in his mouth, Bill waits for us to ask him to sit down at our table, which Dad does. Bill grunts and squishes in on their side. He holds out a fresh pack of Big Red with one red piece sticking out for Elizabeth Ruth.

"Thanks," she says.

"Gotcha!" His face folds into wrinkles as he smiles.

"Ha ha ha, very funny," Elizabeth Ruth says, giving him the empty wrapper back and taking her second, real stick of gum.

Bill tips his baseball cap to me and says, holding out the pack of Big Red, "Evenin' to you, ma'am. Hi there."

I push back against the booth's cushion and give a wave so he knows I heard him. I take a piece of gum. Leaning over the table, he repeats louder, "Hi there!"

I want to hide from him, before he starts pushing on top of me. My eyes shift to Dad, who is watching Caroline lean over the ice cream case, her arm scooping deep down into the vanilla to put into our glasses of root beer.

"She doesn't talk," Hope tells Bill.

"Uh." He laughs like Hope has just told him a joke, then flinches back as paper from a straw whizzes past the side of his head.

"You joker, you," Bill says to Luke. Half-laughing and half-grunting, Bill takes off his cap and reaches over to their booth to place it on Luke's head.

Luke fingers the cap, pressing it tighter to his head.

"Where's the other guy?" Bill asks.

"What other guy?" Dad says sharply. It's like his face has just come into sharp focus.

"That other joker."

No one says anything.

"He had a funny name," Bill says slowly, like he's finally realized something's not right. He smiles with his mouth open, waiting for someone to say something.

Luke's mouth opens, but nothing comes out. The white noise of the air conditioner and the buzz of the freezer fill the silence. Dad's face finally begins to sag, and his eyes lose their glare. Elbows on the table, he props his chin in the palms of his hands. A buffalo nickel glows on the tiles. Elizabeth Ruth picks it up. "Look what I found," she says, holding it to her eye like a silver eye patch.

"So, what's new around town, Bill?"

"Well, I got some photographs of the baseball game the other night I could show you," Bill says, taking out a Star Savers envelope from his knapsack. We pass around the strangely colored photographs. It's the ball game all right, but in the background we can see the frame of his television set and, in some pictures, the control knobs.

"Must've been a great game, Bill," Hope says, giggling.

"Yup, sure was. The Sox beat 'em seven to two."

"Let's feel the old muscle," Dad says to Bill.

"Um, what, Mr. Stone?"

"Like this, Bill." Luke pushes up his sleeve to flex.

"Pshht," John says.

Dad slaps Bill lightly on the arm, repeating, "Show them your muscle, big guy." Dad is the big guy next to Bill. Bill flexes anyway because he doesn't know what else to do. When Caroline comes over with our tray of root beer floats, Bill looks like he's in pain, his face white and grimacing as he squeezes his fist, pumping his upper arm.

Covering their mouths with their Friendly's napkins, Hope and Sarah choke to keep from laughing out loud.

"You okay, Bill?" Caroline asks. "You wanna float, too?"

"Um, yeah, sure," Bubble Gum Bill answers.

After that they all concentrate on spooning the ice cream into their mouths and mixing the melting vanilla into the root beer — except me, keeping an eye on Bill so he doesn't decide to do anything to Elizabeth Ruth like Ray did. Bill sucks up his float carefully in one long gulp. He makes a big clogged-up sucking noise when the lump of ice cream gets stuck in the opening of his straw. We all stare at him.

Root beer explodes out of Luke's mouth, spraying all over the table. "Just drink your drinks," Dad says to Luke and John, without even getting mad. Then he turns to Bill. "Can you beat this, Bill?"

"No, Mr. Stone."

While Dad is paying, I open the long freezer packed with half gallons of ice cream and poke my head inside to feel the cold air rush up on my face. I am running my finger through the layer of frost on a rectangular box with a picture of a shimmering watermelon log when I see Bill slide a pack of Big Red into Elizabeth Ruth's hands wrapped in a knot behind her back. Her whole face glows in the Friendly's lights. I freeze. Through the cold air, rising up from the long freezer, all I see is Ray pushing himself into Elizabeth Ruth. Now Bill is about to do the same. I want it to end.

"You have it. It looks good on you," Bill says, turning to Luke, pushing the Red Sox cap over Luke's forehead. "You're a joker like me."

"It was Ham," Luke whispers. "The one who isn't here."

"Oh, oh, Ham," Bill repeats. "Where's Ham?"

Dad whips around.

"That other guy, Ham, where is he?" He rolls his stupid grinning face at us and duckwalks out with all his contraptions, as

Mum calls them, swaying side to side. Right afterwards, I want him to come back, so we're not all alone with Dad.

Dad's face goes instantly red, and he barges out of Friendly's. We follow him to the car, taking our places before he can start the engine. Seeing Mum's Thomas Merton book under the driver's seat, though, he stands to fling it out the window. It skids across the walkway, coming to a stop in the wood chips beneath a rhododendron bush.

In the front seat, Elizabeth Ruth holds up her buffalo nickel. The humming of the engine through the floor of the car back here, and the wind slapping lightly on my face, feels like the motor of the ferryboat that takes us to Martha's Vineyard moving up through my feet into my body. The sound of seagulls pierces the air. We are speeding through the darkening red and purple sky, past the Cawood dump. *Ask the birds, the birds will know.* They saw everything.

Please stop, Dad, I want to say. I put my hands over my ears, my eyes, my mouth. I squeeze my eyes into black and hold my breath as long as I can, flying in long slow circles. I am flying, I can hear the flutter of my own wings. I don't ever want to go back there to Martha's Vineyard. Ever. Everything goes dark.

"Emily fainted on the way home," Luke yells up the stairs to Mum. "She passed out in the back of the car."

"Shhh," Mum says, rocking Owen in her rocking chair. "Tell me what happened."

Gripping each side of me, Hope and Sarah have me propped between them. "She fainted in the backseat. Right on top of me. At first I thought she was dead," Luke shouts.

"Don't talk like that," Mum says.

"We had to pour cold water on her!"

"We pulled into some guy's driveway. He got it for us," Hope explains.

"What a nice man. Are you all right, Emily?"

I nod, looking at the cracked plate hanging on the wall behind Mum. It's been there as long as I can remember. A pretty woman with long pale hair is riding a huge goose with wings like flower petals. The woman fits right around the arch of the goose's neck. The goose is showing her the way to heaven. Mum says she's going to ride on a goose like this when she goes to heaven.

"You're exhausted," Mum says. "What you need is a good night's sleep."

"We'll put her to bed, Mum," Hope says.

"Those are my good girls. I'll be up in a few minutes."

Mum sits on the edge of my bed, fingering circles on the white spread. Her eyes look somewhere past me, out into the night. "Are you all right?" she asks me. "I don't know when you're going to decide to talk again."

When she says it, though, I can tell she doesn't expect me to. She's used to it. It's like I've won the silent game for good and at least she can count on me to give her some peace and quiet. That's not all, though. I think Mum thinks that because I don't say anything that I can't hear anything.

"Sometimes I think I'll wake up and everything will be like it used to. Oh, look at this," she says, lifting the sheet. "I was going up to change your sheets today and I forgot what it was I was going to do when I got up here. I don't know how many times a day I go upstairs to do something or get something and when I get there, I forget what it was. I just stand there looking around." She shakes her head, the strands of hair falling out from behind her ear. She suddenly looks old and worn-out, sagging everywhere, except around the mouth.

"I don't know what I'm going to do with you, Emily. You know Grandma sent me an article from the paper about a ten-year-old girl who had come all the way from India to have a throat operation at Mass General Hospital so she'd be able to speak. Now, isn't that crazy? Sometimes I think Florida isn't the best place for her. She's getting old so fast. As if I should talk — look at me!" She smiles to herself. She pushes back my hair from my forehead.

In the car, after the funeral, Mum did this — pushed my hair back, but it was covered in sweat and stuck to the palm of her hand.

"I don't think I can do it," she whispered.

"Oh, yes you can. Come on, now." Grandma kept her eyes on the road.

We could see Dad in front of us in the passenger seat of Ernie's beat-up Volvo.

"Why'd he have to come?" Hope asked.

"He's part of the family, Hope," Mum answered.

"Unfortunately," Grandma said, not taking her eyes from the road.

Breathing hard, Mum spun toward her mother. "Ernie loved Ham. He was his godfather."

"Well, he could have at least tried to get to the funeral on time."

Grandma's fingernails were painted silvery white, the same color as her powdery hair, which curled up on her shoulders, and the sparkles that hung from her ears. Nothing was ever out of place on her. She was always straightening our dresses, telling Mum that we needed haircuts. She was always trying to persuade Mum to get a perm, too. Each time she came to visit, it was the same. When she left, Mum would say, "I don't know why it bothers her so much. It's my hair. It's crazy to think of myself with a perm. She was always trying to take control of my life."

On the day of the funeral, when Grandma said it looked like Ernie got his suit at the Salvation Army, Mum exploded for the second time. "He was there when Ham was alive, that's the important thing. He never missed a birthday."

"Once he gave him a rattlesnake," Luke said.

"A rattlesnake?" Grandma asked.

"I hated that snake." Mum half-smiled. She said it like it didn't exist anymore.

"Another time, he gave him a go-cart," Luke said.

"What about the rattlesnake?" Grandma asked. No one answered.

"Was there a rattlesnake in your house?" She turned to Mum.

"Ask Elizabeth Ruth. She's the one who started crying the first time she saw it," Luke said.

"I did not," Elizabeth Ruth cried out.

"Would someone please tell me if there was a rattlesnake in your house?"

"It wasn't alive," Sarah finally answered.

"But it looked like it. It was just about to strike," Elizabeth Ruth added.

"Now, why would you let him keep something like that?" Grandma asked.

"I don't know how he kept it beside his bed," Mum said, still smiling.

"It would have been a lot better if he kept it at home," Elizabeth Ruth blurted out, "but he had to carry it around with him everywhere we went."

"Shut up, Elizabeth Ruth," John said. "Just shut up."

It was true, he took that stuffed snake everywhere, holding the coiled body around the neck, under its open mouth, fangs bared, ready to strike. All the scales started falling off where he held it, and the rattles on the end of its tail had to be taped back on, too.

Ham had set the rattlesnake down once in the breakfast cereal aisle of Star Savers, where a lady Mum knew from church saw it and screamed, and somehow she must have kicked it because it skidded toward the Quaker oats display. Ham screamed, too. One of the rattles cracked when it hit the cardboard display and the snake tipped over on its side. Ham ran to grab it before one of the Star Savers employees coming toward us could get there. The next time we went to Star Savers, Ham had to carry his snake in a paper bag.

I remember watching Mum cover her eyes with her hands in the car, and then we were at the cemetery. The others had gotten out and were waiting in a huddle as the cars pulled up. I could hear birds singing from somewhere close by, and when I looked up, I saw a bluebird, its feathers the color of the sky right before darkness sets in. It perched there without budging.

It was the shock in Grandma's voice that made me turn away — toward where she was pointing at Ernie, who had just thrown himself onto the casket. Dad and the others tried to pull him by the hands and feet, but he clung on. By the time I remembered the bluebird in the tree, it was gone. That's when I knew it was a message from Ham and he was still out there.

Mum is gone, leaving only a sliver of light coming under the door.

I already know from checking the calendar how many days are left before we go to Martha's Vineyard when Hope says, "There are three days left. Everything comes in threes, so we have to be extra careful. See, every day is a balance of good luck and bad luck. So if the day starts off with all bad luck, you can count on some good luck by the afternoon, and the other way around. Everything is a perfect balance in the end, and if it weren't, the whole world would collapse. The sky would cave into the earth." She turns to face Elizabeth Ruth.

"If you really want to be part of the group, Elizabeth Ruth, there's something you need to do first." She's punishing her for not telling us about Ray.

"What?"

"Look inside Mr. Kosik's house and see if he's in there. Emily will go with you to make sure you do it."

"Today?"

"Yes."

"What about Sarah?" Elizabeth Ruth looks like she's going to cry.

"She's going to do something, too. Don't worry."

"What's the matter?" Sarah asks.

"I don't know," Elizabeth Ruth mumbles, wrapping her arms around her legs. "I just don't feel that good."

"Do you want me to go with you, too?" Sarah asks.

"Yes."

"We'll all go," Hope decides. "And I've been thinking we should all start keeping notes on different ideas. First I'm going to cut the damn hose so Dad'll have to get a new one. Then I'm going to get some pictures of Nixon and drop them around his office and the garage. As many as I can. It'll drive him crazy."

"He probably won't even notice," Sarah says.

"Remember when Mum said she felt bad for Nixon? Dad pulled over the car. He was so mad, I thought he was going to make her walk home."

"What if we wrote a letter from Ernie? He's the only one Dad's afraid of," Hope suggests.

"He's too disgusting," Sarah answers. "That's too much, Hope."

"Yeah, he's gross," Elizabeth Ruth says, shivering, holding herself tighter.

Bud trots over, sniffing around us, wagging his stump of a tail. "Woof," Hope says to Bud, who jumps back, his mouth and chin jiggling. "Woof, woof." She eyes him, panting.

A shadow flits by. Sarah laughs and says to Hope, "That's a good dog."

Bud leaps up and barks at the sky. Above us, a bluebird is flying, dipping in and out, over the trees. That's me, flying higher, flashing my wings, flying like Mum's goose to heaven. I feel light as a feather. I laugh with them and not just my shoulders shaking. A sound comes out, something between a whistle and a squeal, like part of a birdsong, flying out of my mouth. They come closer, surrounding me, peering at me, waiting for more.

My sisters listen for another sound, like Mum used to after I first stopped talking. She'd push my chin toward the light to get a closer look. "Open up," she'd say, trying to figure out what was wrong with the inside of my mouth. Once she sprinkled some holy water over my neck.

The bees buzz over the wildflowers. Then Dad's chain saw roars, drowning out everything else. Holding the saw out in front of him, he walks toward the woods to cut down some of the extra trees for John to split into firewood.

We don't look back. We jog lightly over the dry leaves, ducking around the sprawling bushes and snags of overhung trees, holding the branches so they don't fling back at the next person. When we get to the edge of Mr. Kosik's yard, we stop to catch our breath.

"Wow," Elizabeth Ruth says. "There are millions of them." There are birds everywhere, singing, chirping, and darting across the lawn, poking their heads into the boxy houses set on sticks, the plastic tubes and milk containers hung from trees. They are every color and size. The birds are singing so much, their songs make a wall around Mr. Kosik's backyard. There is no place for us, just birds and birds. I wonder why they don't fly away. I wonder if the bluebird is back here.

"Come on," Hope says. "Let's go this way."

We sneak around the lawn to the garage and sidle along the back of his house, keeping our heads crouched beneath the edge of the window, which is opened a couple inches. I follow, watching my feet move step by step through the grass, trying not to shake. The truth is, I'm terrified. Hope peeks through the glass. She frowns, squinting, then motions us up. Dozens of tiny glass horses — appaloosas, bays, spotted, black, strawberry-colored — stand side by side on the windowsill. An empty box lined with tissue paper sits on the table through the window.

Beyond the table is a sink piled high with dirty dishes and a stove so miniature it looks like a play stove with a pretend silver kettle. A doorway leads to an unlit hallway, where Mr. Kosik is smoothing down the front of a navy V-neck sweater. His hands brush over his stomach as he turns to the side, posing in front of the mirror, examining himself like he's inside a dressing room. The light coming through the front door falls on his back, the top of his hump. His gray, puckered face looks like it is tucked into his chest. He frowns, struggling to pull the sweater off, over his hump, as he shuffles toward us with his huge back swallowing him from behind. We drop to the ground. The sound of his feet dragging across the floor becomes louder. He is practically right above us, rustling the tissue paper around inside the box.

"He's putting the sweater back. Don't move," Hope whispers. "Is he crying?"

It's hard to tell over the sound of the wind in the grass and the chirping of the birds.

"We shouldn't spy on him," Sarah says. "He's just trying on a sweater."

"What's so evil about him?" Elizabeth Ruth whispers.

We can hear his feet shuffling away from us.

"Come on, keep your heads down and run."

We don't stop until we reach the small clearing in the empty lot halfway down Willow Street, where we collapse, rolling on the ground, catching our breath. "That was easy!" Hope shrieks.

"No big black dog got us." Elizabeth Ruth laughs.

"I thought the sweater looked good. He's kind of cute," Sarah says, giggling. "He's too old to hurt anyone. And why would he have all those bird feeders if he were so evil?"

"Maybe he's fattening them up to eat," Elizabeth Ruth says.

"Very funny. Who's going to eat a chickadee?" Hope asks.

"You never know."

Way up over the trees, in the deep blue of the sky, an airplane is flying toward a mass of white clouds.

"You know how Robert Robertson's dad killed himself," Elizabeth Ruth says.

We look at her. "Why are you always talking about him?" Hope asks. "Do you like him or something?"

The airplane vanishes into the mountain of clouds.

"No, I mean there wasn't even anything wrong with him, right? I mean, he didn't have a hunchback, or anything."

"Not that I know about," Hope says.

"I don't think so," Sarah answers.

"So, why would he want to kill himself? I don't get it."

Hope shrugs.

"Maybe he felt really bad," Sarah offers.

Elizabeth Ruth doesn't say anything. I wonder if she feels really bad.

"Come on, we better go," Hope decides, brushing herself off. Following her, we cut across the clearing toward Willow Street.

Ray's radio is playing, *I'm as free as a bird now.* I feel the words circle in my mouth, move down through me. *And this bird . . .*

"Cannot cha-a-a-ange," Hope and Sarah sing together, laughing, pointing to Ray in cutoffs halfway up a ladder, also singing along as he paints the second-floor front windows.

"Look. He's practically naked," Sarah says.

"And his face is orange," Hope says, laughing. "I think he's been to the tanning salon." Elizabeth Ruth laughs when they do.

"Let's go home that way," Hope orders, pointing to Ray's backyard. "Nobody's around. Hurry." We're like her little army.

"Well, who do we have here?" Ray asks, holding his brush midair. His chest is spattered with paint. The music keeps playing.

"Why's he so orange?" Sarah whispers to Elizabeth Ruth.

Elizabeth Ruth's face tightens, her lip quivers, and she screams up at him, "Why's your face so orange, Ray?"

"Orange? What do you mean, Liz?" he asks.

"*Liz?*" Sarah and Hope say at the same time, bursting out laughing.

"What's so funny about that?" He frowns, shaking his brush at us. Elizabeth Ruth's hands were grabbing at the air when Ray was pushing himself into her.

"Cuz, I'm as free as a bird," Hope sings. "It's a free country, Ray."

The paint can swings from the hook on the ladder. He turns back, continuing to paint the trim.

"*Liz?*" Sarah repeats, giggling.

"He's so skinny," Hope says. We stare at Ray.

"Her name's not Liz," Hope yells.

Ray whips angrily around to face us beneath his ladder. His mouth opens, about to yell, then he stops, his eyes caught on something at the top of Willow Street. We hear the grunting and chugging before we see the huge truck pulling a long flatbed with a bulldozer chained to it. It all comes careening past Mr. Kosik's, past the empty lot, past us, past the Lawtons', past the O'Dells', and into our driveway. For the first time all summer, I see Mrs. O'Dell stick her white head out of her front door to see what's shaking the street up and down.

We take off through the backwoods, running home to stand in line with everyone else, watching Dad up on the bulldozer. "Look at her," he calls out. "She's a beauty."

"That's right, sir," the man who delivered the bulldozer answers. He leans against the flatbed with one thumb hitched in his jeans and the other flicking the ashes of his cigarette onto the stones of our driveway. "Go ahead, ride her down."

Dad backs down the ramp, jerking to a stop when Bud charges over, barking his head off at the yellow John Deere bulldozer. The truck driver slicks his hair back and takes a deep pull on his cigarette. John leashes Bud, and Dad keeps rolling down the ramp onto the driveway. Mum shakes her head back and forth, her mouth barely moving. "I don't know where he's going to get the money to pay for that."

With a cigarette hanging from the corner of his mouth, the man folds up the ramps on the end of the flatbed, tips his cap to Mum, then drives away as quickly as he came. Dad drives around on his bulldozer, flattening the ground where the trees have been cut, rolling over the Queen Anne's lace, the black-eyed Susans, and the rhubarb along the edge of the woods. We watch John fill the bucket with logs he and Dad have cut down. The logs that are too big go into a pile to be split again. While Dad rides back and forth, clawing up the backyard, digging up clumps of dirt with the bucket and dumping them over the edge of the swamp, John splits logs. He draws his arm back, and, eyeing the top of the log like it's a baseball, he swings the ax over his shoulder and down, slamming the blade into its center. He does this again and again, splitting the logs into pieces that will fit into Dad's woodstove. We stack the wood in piles on the porch. The *chuck, chuck* sound of the ax echoes through the swamp. Bud runs to the end of his leash, yelping and turning in circles around us.

"I can't wait until I'm eighteen," Hope mumbles as she lifts the logs from my arms.

At lunch, Sarah tells Dad her back hurts and gets to stop stacking logs. I get Birdy and put him inside my pocket, where he scratches against my leg, tickling around the brownish pink web forming over the cut on my thigh. After it turns dark, I slip him back in the shoe box beneath my bed.

Dad's bulldozer, which he parked right in our meeting spot, is gleaming under the bright stars back here. Hope and Sarah have just come back from stealing some blue flowers from the O'Dells' garden. "That was so easy," Sarah says, out of breath.

"We could have stolen the whole garden," Hope laughs. "But we only need this many. Hyacinths help during periods of change because they symbolize constancy."

"Uh oh, I think these are hydrangeas, Hope," Sarah says, scrutinizing the blue flowers in her fist. "July is too late for hyacinths."

"No. No, they *are* hyacinths," Hope says loudly. "And they're going to need water. Think you could get us a jar of water, *Liz?*"

"Oh, very funny," Elizabeth Ruth says.

"We didn't know you liked orange men, Liz." Hope forgets all about the flowers. "Can't you see the headline in next week's *Suburban Press?* 'Thirteen-Year-Old Girl Falls in Love with Orange-Faced Divorced Man.'"

"That's so funny I forgot to laugh," Elizabeth Ruth says back.

"Maybe he ate too many carrots," Hope thinks out loud. "Do you two eat carrots together?"

"No, we don't."

"What do you do then?"

"Nothing."

"Nothing?"

"Then why does he call you *Liz?*"

"I don't know."

"Well, he's a little old for you, don't you think?"

"I hate him."

Dad's voice cracks through the air. "Almost time for bed, little piggies." He starts laughing so hard he has to lean on the new pile of logs. "Or I'll blow your house down." He disappears.

"He's drunk." Hope presses herself inside the bucket of the bulldozer, which is like a huge open mouth with yellow, metal teeth. "Sometimes I wish something bad would happen to him," she says. "I mean, something really bad."

"Like what?" Elizabeth Ruth whispers.

I can't imagine our house without Dad. He *is* the strongest one I know.

"You know what I'm going to do?" Hope asks, looking down at her sneakers slipping between the spiky teeth of the bulldozer. "Bring that wooden box in his closet to Martha's Vineyard and open it down there."

Someone swallows her breath. I think it's me.

"If we go," Sarah adds quickly. She is plucking the petals off one of the hydrangeas.

"Yeah, if we go."

Owen begins to cry. Mum's shadow moves across the bedroom. Then there is a piercing screech. Jumping up, we stand in the backyard paralyzed for a minute, staring stupidly at each other, not knowing what to do.

"Was that Mum?" Sarah asks.

"I think so. Come on, let's check," Hope says, sprinting toward the house. Right as we're going in, Dad, with a furious look on his face, flings open the storm door. Using a handkerchief, he carries Birdy by the tail out in front of him.

"Gross. What's that?" Elizabeth Ruth asks.

Dad walks fast, in long steps, past us, to the dark trees, where he hurls Birdy's tiny bony body far into the woods. There isn't even a thump.

"Where'd that come from?" Hope asks.

"Mum found it under Owen's crib," Luke answers.

"Is it a lizard?" Elizabeth Ruth asks.

"Mum thought it was trying to get inside the crib."

"It looked like a little turtle," Sarah says.

"Yuck," Elizabeth Ruth says. "How'd it get inside?"

They shrug. Everyone turns to Hope. "Don't look at me," she says.

"Hope, go see if your mother's all right," Dad says, huffing as he marches by us. They go inside, Sarah carrying the blue hydrangeas.

I squat at the edge of the woods, waiting for Birdy to crawl back to me. As the darkness settles in, I finger the edges of my scab.

Later, Mum comes in to say good night to us. Standing between our beds, she begins, "Thank you, God, for my eyes, ears, nose, and mouth. Thank you for everything you have given me — "

"Mum?" Elizabeth Ruth interrupts.

"What, Elizabeth Ruth?"

"You know how Robert Robertson's dad killed himself?"

"Yes." Mum nods.

"Did anything ever happen to him? Was there anything wrong with him?" Elizabeth Ruth asks. "I mean, he didn't have a hunchback, or anything, right?"

"Not that I know of," Mum answers slowly. "You can't always tell what makes a person feel bad. I guess he didn't have anything to believe in."

"Does Dad feel bad?"

"Once in a while, I guess."

"Did you ever think of killing yourself, Mum?"

"Oh, no. Never," she answers. "But I remember how lucky I am every morning when I get up, then I don't feel bad. I'm so thankful for everything I have — the beautiful sun, the air, the trees, all of you, a warm house with hot water."

"Did Pop kill himself?"

"Of course not," Mum says.

"Would Ernie?"

"Now that's enough, Elizabeth Ruth." Mum closes her eyes and puts her hands together. "Thank you, God, for Mum, Dad, John . . ."

Owen is crying again as I lie in my bed listening for so long I can't remember how long he's been crying or why I can't sleep in the middle of the night. I begin on the top step of the stairs, staring at the blue-green carpet. When I run my fingers through the outside parts where no one steps, tiny grains of sand and dirt dance up into the air. When I look down, the steps are as steep as a cliff, so I grab onto the walls to keep myself from toppling over, and inch down the stairs step by step. Before I go into the kitchen, I click the light on, then off. I sit on the wooden bench and watch the rhododendron petals catching light from somewhere in the dark as they brush up, swishing against the window by Dad's place. Along the windowsill over the sink is a line of tomatoes waiting to turn red.

We used to play the hide-the-nickel game during recess when it was too cold to go outside. Ham and I had to be on the same team because we always knew when the other had the nickel before anyone said anything. That's the way it always was. I read everything in his eyes. My whole world was in there.

If I press the nickel far enough inside my palm, no one will be able to find it. I imagine it is a sharp nail going deeper and deeper into my palm until I am bleeding. What if I started bleeding through my hands, I couldn't yell out, or what if Ray tried to do to me what he did to Elizabeth Ruth? I know his orange face is on the other side of the window and have to hold my breath to make him disappear.

I feel my sisters are looking at me, waiting for me to tell them what happened. I know one thing. I have to hide from all of them because I can't tell them anything. I run to the bathroom and shut the door.

I'm here somewhere. But my eyes won't be still — it seems like they want to escape my face. And I keep hearing Hope and Elizabeth Ruth singing, "Bluebells, bluebells, eevy, ivey overhead, Mum's in the kitchen making bread, Daddy's in the parlor, cutting off his head. How many chops did he receive?" When I close my eyes, I see a huge shapeless man chopping and chopping, but his head doesn't fall off. Dad's not crazy. Dad's asleep upstairs keeping us safe from everything. Daddy, don't go anywhere.

I hit my forehead against the tiles, going *thump thump* like a heart. I open my eyes. There I am. Emily Stone.

I slide off the bathroom counter to walk into the living room. Everything's so quiet, I'm afraid to move. I stare at the reading lamp in here with a British soldier Ham outlined on the shade in Magic Marker, marking around his stiff red-and-white coat, along the tall sword clenched in his hands, around the hard helmet strapped under his chin. Mum tried to scrape off the marker, but it wouldn't come off, and she finally gave up. He's not coming back. Ham's never coming back. What am I going to do? I wish I could be outlined in marker because I feel like I'm not here.

It's so quiet, I wish Owen would start crying again. If I threw a rock at the chicken coop, maybe the chickens would think it was sunrise and begin their morning cackling and scratching and would wake everyone up. What I do is pull my hair into a pony-tail so none of the loose strands brushes against my face and tickles me. I find a piece of paper and pen and go into the heater room. I pass by Mum's calendar without looking at it. I know there are two days left before we leave. Wrapping my johnny around me, I squeeze myself right in beside the heater. On my paper I write, "Ham, where are you?"

My pen skids up the paper when Dad's alarm goes off, the radio man's deep voice blaring out about another record hot day. It's 5:15 A.M. and I know enough to get back into bed before we all have to get in the lineup.

I lose track of time, but I know it's almost time to go. I don't dream at night, but in the day I hide somewhere and dream all the time of our house on Martha's Vineyard with the speckled shingles and the smell of seawater everywhere. In my dreams I sleepwalk through the rooms, my arms straight out in front of me, feeling the photos along the wall. Ham's face is behind the glass. He opens his mouth to smile at me. *Here I am, Ham,* I say. I want to get closer, but I can't find him anywhere. Then Dad is chasing me because I've done something wrong. But I'm not fast enough. First I hear the glass smashing and then I see myself falling through it, a black sea of broken glass. I don't feel anything.

Mum finds me asleep in the laundry pile. "There you are. For heaven's sake, Emily," she says, "these are clean — I'm going to have to wash everything again now.

"What am I going to do with you?" She shakes her head, gazing out the window, her eyes on the chicken coop. Then she puts her hand on my forehead. "Are you all right, Emily? You're hot, but I suppose everyone is hot these days.

"Last summer was the worst, though. I'll bet we never get another summer like that.

"Remember when Ernie stopped on the way home and walked straight into the ocean? That suit was awful. I think it looked better wet, fit him better. He doesn't even know how to swim either. Just kept on walking out until the water was up to his neck and then he walked back. Grandma threw a fit because half the town was watching him and if they didn't figure out how crazy he was before this, they did then." She's forgotten all about the laundry. I realize that Mum can't stop thinking about the funeral. Every time she sees me, she's like a broken record with it.

Mum pads into the kitchen, humming as she sets the dishes on the table. Upstairs Dad's footsteps are heavy and quick as he goes into the bathroom to clear his throat. "Auughh." He spits, then coughs, clearing his throat. Upstairs the toilet flushes once, then again, and there are footsteps treading over the carpet, which I match to the person by the weight pressing on the floor above.

Mum clicks the burner on the stove and puts a metal lid on top of the pot filled with Dad's hot oatmeal. She fills a second pan with hot water to boil his three eggs, which she has collected from the chicken coop. She has risen early in order to get everything ready. Today is the day. Everyone knows we have breakfast first, the lineup second, and third, get in the car to take the ferryboat to Martha's Vineyard. Everyone will go, except me.

Pit-pat go Mum's slippers across the kitchen floor as Dad's heavy steps come down the stairs. His chair scrapes across the linoleum. The eggs jiggle against the side of the pan in the boiling water, a bowl is set down, and Dad spoons oatmeal into his mouth. Slurp. Breath. Slurp.

Everyone else whispers at the top of the stairs, then all come down at once. "Good morning," they say softly.

Mum answers, "Good morning."

Dad eats his cereal. Folding my knees tighter, stirring up the thick dust, I squeeze further down, closer to the pipes behind the heater. I have found the best spot in the house. Someone would have to look good and hard to find me here.

"Where's Emily?" Dad suddenly asks, stopping the sound of spoons hitting the sides of the cereal bowls, quieting everyone.

"I don't know."

"I never saw her."

"Well, where did she sleep?" Dad shouts next, slamming his fist on the table. Mum gasps, then catches herself. I thought they wouldn't notice. I thought they'd just leave without me.

"I don't know." Elizabeth Ruth's voice is shaking.

"Where is she?" he asks louder.

"I don't know, either," Sarah answers, soft and far away. "She didn't sleep in our room."

"Maybe she slept in their room," Elizabeth Ruth says, nodding toward Luke.

"No, she didn't," Luke says right back.

"She's got to be here somewhere. Where can she be? We'll find her. Eat up your cornflakes before they get all soggy," Mum tells them. Someone shakes the box of cornflakes.

"Hope, where is your sister?" Dad yells.

I wonder if his face is white or red, and if his lips are pulled tight across his face.

"I don't know," Hope yells right back. "She hasn't been sleeping very well. Maybe she fell asleep somewhere in the house, I don't know." Nobody tells Hope not to yell, that it's against the rules unless you're Dad. How does Hope know I haven't been sleeping?

They don't say anything. I'm waiting for them to forget about me and just go to Martha's Vineyard. I can't understand why they're going to so much trouble. My legs are numb from not moving and the sweat is running in small streams down my back. Even Owen knows something is wrong and starts shrieking.

"That's it," Dad says, spitting the words like stones from his mouth. "Nobody knows where she is, no one goes anywhere until we've searched the entire house upside down." He divides them into groups to search upstairs, downstairs, and outside the house.

I guess they better find me now or everyone's going to get it. Now look what I've done. I don't want to go. I can't go back there. Please don't make me.

Someone is pulling everything out of the wooden lockers Dad built in the heater room to store our coats, mittens, boots, rain jackets, bats, balls, jump ropes, and everything. *Clunk, clunk.*

"Emily, where are you? You have to come with us," Luke says.

"Maybe she's dead." It's Luke again. He drops whatever he's holding.

"Well if she was, no one would know because she doesn't talk." He starts laughing. Why are you talking to yourself, I want to ask.

Tap, tap, tap. I knock against the cement wall behind me. Everything is so crowded and hot in here, I feel like I'm trapped. I can't feel anything. I see my arm reaching out and then Luke is there, his bright face peering down at me. He pulls back quickly, breathing in gulps, whispering, "I thought you were someone else." His face crumbles.

I feel like I can see myself rising. I'm not Ham.

"I found her. I found Emily," Luke announces to Dad, who steps into the heater room.

Catch me, try and catch me, I want to say, because I'm not really here. I'm flying away from everybody. The air swishes over my body, wet with sweat. Feathers brush the edges of my lips. I'm flying through my mouth.

Luke stands back as Dad pulls me by my arm to the end of the long kitchen table — before I turn invisible. My sisters peek into the kitchen. They look at each other funny, trying to find me. No one can see me, except Dad. Dad tells them to hurry up and pack the car so we can leave in ten minutes.

He squeezes the Star Savers chocolate syrup into the tall glass of milk and stirs. Then he carries my chocolate milk over to the sink and plops something into it. Dad smiles so wide, I can see the inside of his mouth. "Thatta girl, drink it right down. Good girl."

I do, I drink it all down, tipping the last chocolate bubbles and the three small white pills right down.

I'm really flying. The wind is carrying me, lifting me up and down through the salty air. The air brushes against my cheeks as I dip and dive, searching for Ham. I call him. I won't climb out the window like I did after the funeral, I promise. My eyes are open, but I can't even budge!

After the funeral, when we were driving back from the cemetery, the wind lifted my white dress like a sail, gathering it around my waist as I perched on the edge of the window, ready to fly. I was about to push myself through the window. I was so close to the sky, I could feel myself soaring, a fingertip away. All I wanted to do was get out there where he was. Then someone, Elizabeth Ruth, I think, screamed my name, and I stopped for a second, long enough for Hope to pull me back and strap me with her arms. Grandma stopped the car. Then Mum slid into the backseat and rocked me back and forth, begging me, "Please don't do that again, Emily. It's bad enough as it is. Say you won't do it again."

Dad, who was driving with Ernie, beeped the horn. Mum just

kept holding me so tight it hurt. He and Ernie got out of the Volvo.

"Baby, what's going on?" he demanded, motioning to the cars lined up along the seawall behind him. "Everyone's waiting for us."

Dad began pacing beside the car. "Is someone going to answer me?"

"You saw her," Ernie told him. "What do you think happened?"

"I'm not asking you," Dad yelled. He flung his coat over his shoulder. "Look at all of them — waiting for us, for God's sake."

"Come on, let's go home now," Grandma said in her clipped voice. "Shut the door, Hope, and let's keep going."

"Emily, look at me," Dad shouted. "Right now."

Mum smoothed my dress over my bare legs and I looked at Dad, right into his eyes, squinting down on me. I knew then what he had done. I saw him behind Ham at the bridge before he jumped. The current was pulling out to sea. It wasn't until we were on the other side of the railing that I knew Ham couldn't jump. Ham clung to the railing. The blue-green swirls of water turned black. Everything was turning, like in a dream.

"I'll jump," I said.

When Dad said one, two, I spread my arms and flew off the edge of the bridge when Dad said three. I didn't look back, but I saw, in that second of flying, a shadow slip behind me, I know I did. And I heard my name just once, the sound of *Emily.*

Whatever Dad saw in my eyes made his mouth open as he stepped back, into Ernie.

"What's the matter with you?" Ernie asked, pushing him away. "Wake up, Donald."

Dad turned to face the line of cars pulled over on Beach Road, then slowly answered, "Nothing, nothing. I guess I'm wiped out, that's all. I'll drive the Oldsmobile. I'll drive them home." He wiped the back of his hand over his brow and got into the car. That was the first day Dad gave me those little white pills.

They were like the heat melting into me.

We are on our way to Martha's Vineyard. I will be a good girl, Dad. I nod, waiting for that wave of calm to settle in. This is what I've been waiting for, a tingling numbness. The blue sea and sky go on forever. Soon Ham will be back. When I find him, I'm going to tell him everything.

6

I don't know how long I have been sleeping when I wake and find myself in a room filled with sunlight streaming through the curtainless windows. I don't remember the car ride or the ferry or anything. I don't know who saw the Bourne Bridge first. The sun hurts my eyes. I remember Mum singing, someone hammering, a door creaking open, the foghorn bellowing, and there was a dog barking somewhere in the night, unsettling the quiet. Or maybe it was a dream, I can't tell anymore.

Everything looks the same.

There is the sand-colored wicker couch and the coffee table with the glass top covering our collection of shells we sprinkled with a layer of beach sand. I run my finger along the clean top, not picking up a trace of dust. There is the cobalt blue table and the sand dollar linoleum floor, cold beneath my feet right now. Dirty cereal bowls are piled up beside the sink. Everything is exactly as it was, but emptied out somehow. The walls are bare. The framed photographs Mum had lined up on the wall are no longer there, but I can still see the outline of where they hung. No photographs of Ham, Dad said, and knocked them off the wall.

Nothing is on the walls. With my finger, I follow the paths of lines up and back along the hallway, over the small holes and their cracks like crooked veins running through the stained yellow. They seem to tilt closer to me, cracking as they run all along the baseboard to Dad and Mum's bedroom. I stand there in front of the door. My head is so heavy, I don't know what it is I don't want to see in their bedroom. The whole wall cracks, spidering outward. My mouth opens, but nothing comes out. The crack covers the whole wall.

"Good morning." Mum's voice rings out from the front yard.

I step toward where she is. I smell the salt water from the lagoon. The cracks disappear, the walls become instantly clean and white. I turn away, open the refrigerator, and pour myself a glass of orange juice. It's so sweet and pulpy, I drink three glasses. Nothing ever tasted so good.

Mum takes a clothespin from her apron pocket to clip a dishrag onto the clothesline. Dark strands of hair blow against her pink cheeks as she bends to smell a tiger lily growing up along the clothesline pole. I am walking toward her when Miss Patrick, who has lived across the street for at least forty years, comes from behind the hedge, over the lawn, heading in the same direction.

On her second-floor outdoor porch, Miss Patrick has propped a mannequin dressed in a billowing creamy-colored gown, with a pink scarf tied under the chin, the ends blowing either out toward the sea or back to the house, depending on the wind. "She's a bride dressed for her wedding. She's waiting for someone who's probably sunk to the bottom of the ocean, to come back and marry her," Hope told us.

"She doesn't know how lucky she is," Mum said.

Mum puts her arms around Miss Patrick and begins chatting away as if we never left Oak Bluffs at all, laughing out loud as she hangs our T-shirts and socks on the line. They go on as if everything was like it used to be. I glare at them from behind the hedge that closes in on our yard. But hearing Mum laugh makes me come closer. No one else is here except Owen in the carriage next to the clothesline.

I step quietly over to Mum and lean into her waist. She just kisses my forehead, then brushes my long hair down my back with her fingers, not mentioning how long I've been sleeping or anything.

"Hello, Emily." Miss Patrick wrinkles up her face at me.

"Hello," she repeats, waiting for me to say something to her.

"She's tired. Yesterday was a big day," Mum answers quickly.

"And that must be your newest." She peeks into the carriage.

"Yes, that's our Owen," Mum says.

"Oh, he's beautiful. You haven't gotten" — she leans closer, hesitating — "a dog, have you? I could have sworn I heard a dog barking last night." Her thick eyeglasses slip down onto the edge of her nose, her beady eyes drilling into Mum's. Everyone who lives here knows everything about everyone else. It's much worse than Cawood because here the houses are closer together and all the neighbors walk around, saying hello to each other, comparing gardens and talking about the weather.

"Well, yes, we have a nice bulldog. He's a little yappy, but he doesn't bark at night. He's never done that." Mum sounds hurt.

"That's odd, it wasn't the Livingstons' either. Poor old Bozo is about to be put to sleep," Miss Patrick replies, stuffing her hands deep into the pockets of her wraparound skirt. "We haven't had a barker around here in quite a while." She pushes her thick glasses back up on her nose and searches our yard.

"Bud must be with Donald," Mum answers.

I know I heard barking, too, interrupting my thick sleep, but it seems like so long ago. My shoulder fits like a puzzle piece underneath Mum's arm, my side into her hipbone.

After Miss Patrick leaves, Mum says, "She acted like I was hiding a dog around here. As if one isn't enough." She decides to air out the house, wash the curtains, mop the kitchen floor, and wipe down the windowsills. I follow her, humming, from room to room, stirring up dust.

"I'm going to clean this house inside out," she tells me. I stay close by her so none of the walls starts cracking or pressing down on me.

As soon as the others get back in the Oldsmobile, I go with Hope, Sarah, and Elizabeth Ruth into the shed, where they have three cots set up to sleep on. "I'm glad you finally woke up," Sarah says to me. "Mum said you were exhausted from not sleeping the whole night before."

"You didn't miss anything," Hope says loudly. "We got the grand tour, Edgartown and up-island, where all the big houses are," she says mockingly. "Boresville."

"You missed this," Elizabeth Ruth says, turning to proudly stroke up the length of her legs, her belly and her arms, over her wrists and along her fingers to her knucklebones. Her skin is as smooth as egg whites.

"You look like a smelt fish," Hope says. I know she means the silver ones that glitter like they are covered in clear oil as they skit over the waves in the moonlight. "I don't know why you did that, Elizabeth Ruth. When it grows back, it's going to be twice as thick."

"Hirsute," Sarah says, "that's what you'll be."

"Her gorilla suit, you mean," Hope corrects her.

"I like it," she states. "Here was the hardest." She pulls up her skirt so we can see the outline of her pale hipbones. "I just have my eyebrows left."

"Whatever you do, don't shave your eyebrows, Elizabeth Ruth. You'll look worse," Hope says.

"Do you think *he'll* notice?" she asks us.

"Dad?" Sarah cracks sunflower seeds open in her mouth over and over, spitting the seeds into her fingers to put in a pile of wet cracked shells beside her on the shed floor.

"Yeah," Elizabeth Ruth asks us again, "do you?" The tiny wisps of hair above her lip have been shaved, too.

"Who cares?" Hope says, leaping off the cot and, clutching my hand, points it at the door and marches me Russian-style toward the back of the shed. I drag behind her, so she lifts me and swings me around, my bare feet hitting against the old Mobil oilcans, sending dirty red Pegasus flying to the ground. Then Hope pins me flat on my back on the cot and starts tickling me under the arms, the ribs, and everywhere, telling me, "Come on, laugh louder."

I do. I am. I'm going to explode. It feels like all the blood is rushing right up under the lid in the back of my throat, holding everything down. *Hope!* I'm about to scream out, but I have to hold it all in before I tell them everything, including the cracks that split down the wall today when Mum wasn't there.

With one hairless arm stretched in a diagonal from one side of the doorframe to the other, Elizabeth Ruth stands watching us. "Do you think Ray's wondering where we are?" she asks Hope.

"Who cares about stupid, skinny Ray?" Hope says back, stretching out on the cot, folding her long brown arms behind her head. "What's that smell?"

Elizabeth Ruth sighs and throws a paper bag at me. "We got you these this morning." Inside are malted milk balls, my favorite.

"It smells like a fire," Sarah says. "Open the door."

Elizabeth Ruth pushes open the shed door, which falls off its hinges, and we can see dark strips of smoke waft around our shed as Dad drops sticks of dry bamboo one by one into the flames, crackling as they burn our backyard to stubble. The grass around the bamboo has turned a copper color.

"Look," Sarah cries, pointing to a family of baby skunks filing out of the bramble away from the fire. "There are six of them. I thought they never came out in the day."

"It's skunk hour," Hope says. "You know what that means. Be careful what you wish for." Each of her words is like a rock dropping into still water. I wonder what bad luck the skunks are going to bring.

I slip through the smoke to sit on the front doorstep and eat my malted milk balls one by one. I push each one from one side of my mouth to the other, softening the chocolate with my tongue until it slowly melts off and the malted ball starts to dissolve. When I can't wait any longer, I break the ball in two and suck on the halves, seeing how long I can make them last.

"What do you have there, champ?" Dad shouts. When he lowers his sunglasses on his sunburned nose to get a better view of me, his eyes look even brighter blue than before. I hold up my paper bag for him to see the malted milk balls.

"We're going to have a good time this week, do you hear me?" he says, placing his heavy hand on top of my head for a moment and then passes me, first him and then his shadow. "Am I right or am I right?"

When he leans against the door of the Oldsmobile in his white alligator shirt and new plaid shorts belted at the waist with a cloth belt, he looks like someone in the movies. If we were in the movies, I'd have to get out of the scene — away from the sunny spot in front of our beach house — because they never have people who don't talk in the movies.

Elizabeth Ruth could be in the movie, I think, as she skips by, flouncing her hips, her short hair bouncing. He pulls her close to him to ask, "Who's the king of the island, Ruthy?"

"You are." She tilts her head, squinting into the sun to answer him. Her body is shining up at him, but I don't think he notices that she has shaved off all of her hair.

As we march into the brightness of the A&P the next morning, I see Elizabeth Ruth's bare arms and legs glisten with the oil she has rubbed on herself. Mum's been so busy going over her list for our special dinner tonight to celebrate Dad's newest invention, she hasn't noticed that Elizabeth Ruth has shaved herself everywhere. Mum's just happy that Dad's in such a good mood. Nobody asks Mum why she took the long way to get here instead of going down Beach Road past the bridge.

"Rolls, green beans with butter, corn on the cob, baked fish," Mum says to herself again.

A silver-haired lady steps out from behind the register to coo at Owen and touch his dark head. I really don't know how anyone could act so silly over a baby. "Oh, he's adorable. Welcome back, Mrs. Stone. How was your winter?" Her eyes travel down to Mum's small hand and the stubs of her knobby fingers. I tug on Mum's dress to pull her away. The meat man signals to someone by pointing over to us. It feels all of a sudden as if everyone is eye-balling us. They all know what happened. They know what I did.

"Fine, just fine, thank you." Mum smiles back at the cashier, which makes me tug at her harder.

"How long are you here for?"

"A couple of weeks."

"You must have brought the good weather with you."

"I hope so." Mum nods.

"Good to have you back, Mrs. Stone." The woman smiles, but I know she's lying.

I push the carriage forward. Running her good finger over her dry lips, Mum says, "Oh, I forgot my lipstick. Oh well."

They're watching me. I know they're staring at me, thinking,

There's Emily Stone, the girl who killed her brother. I don't need a mark on my face like Cain, my face is my mark. I wish I could be like Mum, not letting anything bother her. I want to hide from them and not let their staring bother me.

Mum picks up a can of brown beans, reads the price, and shakes her head, saying, "Outrageous. At Star Savers, this would be seventy-nine cents."

Luke kneels in the candy aisle to open a bag of Milky Ways or Mounds bars. Elizabeth Ruth follows Hope over to the lobster tank beside the stacked loaves of Wonder bread. Hope stands on the tips of her toes, reaching her hands over the edge of the tank near the bubbling water. Sarah walks to the spinning rack of romance books. No one else seems to mind that everyone in the A&P is staring and whispering at us. I hang on to the side of our cart, as if that will hide me.

When we get to the end of the meat counter, I hear, "Want a little taste of heaven?" A lady with shining angel wings attached at the shoulders hands out sample crackers with a swirl of white cheese. "It's new. Heavenly cheese spread," she tells us.

"Oh, thank you." Mum takes a "taste of heaven" on a napkin and I take just a napkin, which I tear in half, wad up, and press into my ears. The angel wings flutter as the woman holds out the plate piled with heaven to the next passing customer. She smiles as her lips move to form the words, "Want a little taste of heaven?"

With Owen propped on her right hip, Mum reaches up for Campbell's soup, Ragu spaghetti sauce, or gherkin pickles. I watch her lips moving, as she frowns or shrugs, deciding which items to place in the cart before we push on. If I talked, I'd tell everyone shopping around us to stop staring at Owen and Mum and her stubby hand. No one notices me anymore, because I'm invisible. No one can get near me. Not Hope, Sarah, Elizabeth Ruth, Luke, Mum — nobody. Someone is trying, though.

Someone is following me down the fruit and vegetable aisle, past the heads of lettuce, sliding behind the piles of Idaho potatoes, inside the husks of ears of corn. I'm afraid to turn around and see him jumping, turning to stop, then falling, his head hanging all wrong. I walk toward the apples and oranges. He's close by. Where are you, Ham? In the reflection on the silver shelf above the red delicious apples I see him. His skin is a bluish color and his mouth is red. His eyes are closed and his mouth is a hole.

He isn't talking. *Ham.*

I whip around to finally see him.

Only Mum is there, peeling back the soft husks on the corn to check if the first kernels are small and whitish yellow. In the reflecting silver behind me, I see myself, my wild eyes staring back at me. *Where are you, Ham?* I run past the peaches and plums, blueberries and bananas. My ears buzzing, I search the lettuce, beans, cucumbers, and avocados until I have circled the vegetable aisle twice. I run my fingers over the green and red grapes, the honeydew. Finally, I slow down. Dizzy, I pick up a bruised red delicious apple, mushy and leaking from the inside out. I bite down on the fleshiest part of my forearm until my arm is bruised like the apple and hurts enough so the rest of me stops hurting. There are two perfect half circles that make an oval, showing the indents of each tooth marked by tiny red dots.

"Emily," Mum calls, "I'm going to get in line. Come on."

I don't watch Mum or Owen or any of them anymore, now that I have my arm to look at.

Mum drives the long way home to avoid the bridge again. She pretends not to hear Hope say, "Dad drove by it already."

"I can't believe Dad let us get whatever we wanted at the store yesterday," Elizabeth Ruth says. "Remember when we went to Friendly's and he said, 'Nothing fancy?'"

Hope twirls her finger beside her ear, meaning, "someone's crazy." She asks, "What's the new invention, Mum?"

"He hasn't told me yet. All I know is that he's been waiting to get down here to try it out. Guess we'll find out tonight," she answers, taking a deep breath of sea air. "Hmm, smell, it's so beautiful here, isn't it?" No one answers her.

When we drive past the hospital, I look out to the sea, remembering the glossy, speckled tiles, the sharp pine smell of the floor cleaner, the soft buzz of televisions, carts rolling down the hall, the aqua curtains dividing the rooms in two.

Ping, ping, the ends of the green beans I'm snapping hit the sides of the metal bowl. Hope stops peeling cucumbers to whisper to Sarah, "Elizabeth Ruth said she heard a dog barking outside our window last night."

"The skins have all the vitamins and minerals. You really should leave these on." Sarah points to the naked cucumber. Then she whispers back, "Do you think she really did?"

"You never know with her."

"And now it's a four-to-two game," the baseball announcer booms out from the living room. It's the first game of a doubleheader. "Here's the three-two pitch, and he whacks it into center field for a base hit. The runners move to second and third and the bases are loaded."

"I'm Carl Yastrzemski," Luke yells out.

"I am."

"I'm going to get a grand slam. Yes!" Luke yells back at himself.

Dad shuffles into the kitchen, opens the refrigerator, takes out a tall can of Busch, and cracks it open. His clothes still smell of smoke. "Those are my girls," Dad says to us, getting supper ready. Throwing his head back, he gulps the cold beer along with some aspirin or Tums or both, burping as he walks back into the living room.

"It's the top of the ninth and the Red Sox have taken the lead. The first pitch is low. Ball one." The crowd is roaring behind the announcer, who shouts out, "And the pitch gets away. It goes right through his legs —"

"What a bologna artist. A bunch of losers." Dad hisses. A minute later, he asks, "Who wants a sip? Whoa! Just a sip there, buddy."

"Oh, great" — Hope rolls her eyes at us — "I hope they don't lose the game." Hope is ripping the husks off the corn and Sarah is chopping carrots and celery when Hope points out the window over the sink to Elizabeth Ruth sitting in the red oak in the front yard. "We have to find out if Elizabeth Ruth is going crazy or not." Sarah nods. I hope I'm not crazy like she is. Dad better not see her up there, that's all I can say. Now is when I'm glad I can't tell them anything about Ray or Elizabeth Ruth wiping her private with leaves, or anything.

"Let's find out if she really heard a dog barking." Hope turns to me. "Can you watch outside the shed and tell us if you hear anything? I mean, you can just write everything down, okay? Will you do it?"

I nod and close my eyes. White dots in the black, like the lights strung together into Japanese lanterns hung along the trim of all the gingerbread houses on Illumination Night, the night they light up everything around the tabernacle by our house. All the lights blur into one.

My eyes fill up and I think I'm going to cry, until I hear Dad clearing his throat as he reaches for another beer from the refrigerator. *Ping, ping,* go my green beans. No one's going to catch me crying, especially not him.

"Strike three, he's outta there," the announcer tells us. "First game of the doubleheader's over, folks."

"Damn idiots," Dad says, whacking the TV.

It's dead quiet and I'm still waiting for the Red Sox to win, still waiting to hear, "It's way out here, this baby's way up there, it's gone." Over the Green Monster, into outer space. Or balk, couldn't they call a balk or something?

Dad leaves, slamming the back door. Next thing Luke walks in, his head rolling from one side to the other like a top spinning. "Damn idiots," he says laughing.

"Have you been drinking, Luke?" Hope mumbles, swinging her honey brown hair across her shoulders, turning her back to him. Luke yanks a fistful of Hope's hair as hard as he can and bolts out the kitchen door. As if a storm has gathered in Hope, she slams the ear of corn she is peeling down on the counter and chases after him. The kitchen door slaps and flaps.

From the straw doormat that reads "Home Is Where the Heart Is," Sarah and I watch Hope chase Luke down the street. Someone passing in an old pickup truck toots his horn at Hope. She flips him the finger, then turns back home, with Luke following from a safe distance.

Mum's singing one of her church songs as she carries the laundry basket from the clothesline. Her eyes are shining like the ice cubes in Sarah's glass of ginger ale.

As he backs out of his work shed, Dad grunts, panting, with Bud at his side. When he sees Mum, he steps up and puts his arm tight around her waist and says, "How about making your old man a little drink?" The light goes out of Mum's eyes.

From the other side of the lawn, Elizabeth Ruth starts screaming like a crazy person. Luke is chasing her with a black rubber eel, squirming in the air like it's alive, dangling it behind her. The hair on Sarah's arm stands straight up.

"Hey, what's going on over there?" Dad calls loudly from the shed.

Plunk, Luke drops the eel back into the silver bucket for holding Dad's bait. Reeling slightly from side to side, Luke doesn't see Dad coming up behind him. We all stop frozen. "Nothing's going on, Donald Duck," Luke says, chuckling to himself.

"Don't you Donald Duck me, mister," Dad says, trotting up to Luke, winding his right foot back. He kicks Luke hard on the behind. Luke cries out, grabbing at the back of himself, running a little, catching himself, almost falling. "Or I'll give you something to laugh about. Now, beat it," Dad calls out, his hands balled into fists as he kicks Luke again with his new loafers. From where he lies on the grass, Luke looks up at us as if he wants us to do something. Like we should have caught him or something before he fell. Then he runs somewhere behind the house.

"It's good we have a hedge around the yard." Sarah sighs.

I can't remember what day it is. There isn't a calendar down here. The sound of the foghorn blasts across the water along the harbor, where clouds are piling up like white stones. Are they going to fall on me like they did to Elizabeth Ruth in her dream?

"When's chow, baby?" Dad calls to Mum in the kitchen. The sun keeps shining on Dad's speckled white hair, whiter against his sunburned face.

"About an hour," she answers, carrying out his drink.

I run around back to find Luke with his head between his knees. Everything smells of smoke back here except for the beer on his mouth. When he lifts his head, Luke wipes his runny nose on his arm.

We watch the black stubby ground, not saying anything until he blurts out, "Remember the time we went to the baseball game and Ham almost got Yaz's autograph? But he didn't have a pen with him, just his snake."

"'Sorry kid' — that's what he said." I watch Luke turn his head from right to left. "Mum gave us a dollar each."

"And you ate horse meat, remember? John said it was hamburger."

"I never ate horse meat."

"Did so. You started crying."

"I ate three hot dogs that day. And they won, the Red Sox."

Who are you talking to, Luke? That's what I want to ask him. The hot air hisses. The soot is warm between my toes. I try to flick this strange tingling off of me.

The light flitters across Luke's eyes. Then Dad's whistle blows sharply, even though we weren't supposed to have any lineups on this vacation. We scramble up too fast and almost knock each other over. I slide my feet into my sneakers, Luke grabs my hand, and we run like we're running away from someone back here.

Ham, that's who Luke has been talking to. Past the burnt stubble back here, I see the dock where we always used to go. My heart skips a beat and I know Ham's going to meet me there. Soon.

7

"Monkey, monkey man doing the hula hula hula dance," Elizabeth Ruth sings softly as we stand in a line, arms at our sides, toes lined up on the edge of the driveway, waiting for Dad. What's taking Dad so long? We aren't behind the hedge, and Oak Bluffs isn't like Cawood, where no one can see us waiting in a stupid line. Here everyone will know. Everyone will think we're crazy.

"Monkey man, sandman, monkey man, sandman," Elizabeth Ruth keeps singing softly. "When the sun goes down, the sandman comes, to sprinkle sand in the eyes of his little ones." I elbow her to warn her to be quiet. She glares back at me and sings it again.

There he is, hugging his tall glass with his arms folded across his chest. Maybe this invention really is the one we've all been waiting for. But that's what we thought about the Tiger Soap, the woodstove, the Supergrow Instant Fertilizer, the nautical brass lantern and clock, and all the others. What if Dad can't make another Magic Rose? From the way he's standing there as solid as a statue, I think this one's going to be a success. It better be.

"Tonight's the big test, kids. She's going to fly tonight," he says. Marking the low grass with the heel of one of his loafers, Dad tells John, "I need a hole dug right here."

Starting toward the toolshed, John mutters under his breath, "A bunch of crap." The rest of us watch Dad set his drink down and drag two wooden sawhorses over onto the edge of the lawn. He walks off to the side of the shed and comes back carrying a long wooden pole, setting either end on the horses. With the heel of his boot, John presses the shovel deep into the brownish green lawn, scooping the dirt out into a small pile beside the hole.

"When it's all set up, this is going to be the mast, see?" Dad pauses. "I'm going to rig up the sail and flag with my special reflecting sheaths to reflect the moonlight," he explains. "So you can sail at night or fish, say. She's going to turn fishing around. Just you wait and see." Dad runs the palms of his hand along the polished wood of the mast.

"Hope and Sarah, you can go ahead inside and help your mother finish getting ready for supper," Dad orders. As Hope turns to march away, she grins at us, tossing her hair back.

"Luke, go get my saw like a good kid," Dad tells him, giving him a push on the back. We watch John digging, sliding his hand down the handle of the shovel, scooping into the earth. When Luke returns, holding out the handsaw, Dad says, "Okay, Emily, now I need you to hold the legs of the horse steady for me."

Automatically I walk over to the wooden horse where the mast is balanced and squeeze my hands around the legs of the horse and watch my fingers turn white. From here I see no one; they have left me, crouching beneath Dad, whistling long then short.

Chuck, chuck is the sound of the saw. *Chuck, chuck, chuck.* I can taste the sawdust, the sawdust and dirt and Dad's whistling filling the air around me. I wonder if he is watching me.

My shoelace holes on the canvas tops of my sneakers fill with sawdust. It's hard to breathe. I keep my knees bent and fingers wrapped around the wooden legs of the horse. When I look up, I see the sun spreading itself like pink legs across the sky. Dad's mouth is a tight line as he saws back and forth. He cuts to the rhythm of *chuck, chuck*.

No one was supposed to see. I saw Ham fall. He didn't want to jump. Dad made him. That's what happened. *Chuck, chuck* — his arm goes in and out, cutting, sawing through the wood. I grip the legs of Dad's sawhorse to hold myself steady. The birds were cooing, flapping overhead. *It wasn't my fault.*

I look at Dad. Don't look at Dad. It's too late. I was falling, too, through the glass. Dad's bottle smashed into thousands of pieces. He was behind me, Dad was, when I fell through all the glass. Something hit me on the back of the head. Everything went black, like in my dream. In my dream, Dad is always chasing me. What did I do, Dad? What did I do wrong? I look up at him, cutting back and forth, his mouth a grimace, his arm sawing. *Chuck, chuck. Chuck, chuck.*

I saw them. Mum's face was screaming into the floor. Dad stood over, pushing her face into the floor. What was it Mum kept on saying? She was curling away from him as he pressed harder into her, his hand like a mask on her face, covering her mouth, covering her eyes. This is what I saw. Dad didn't look at her. He doesn't look at me now. I grip the legs of the wooden horse to stop myself from falling through the broken glass. *Chuck, chuck.*

"I don't want another baby," she said when Dad put his hand on her face. His face is red and lined with wrinkles, and beads of sweat run down his cheeks. She was trying to curl away from him, but he wouldn't let her. The dust rises and falls around me, making me choke. It looked like Mum's face was falling off of her. My hands slip down the legs of the horse.

I can't move from where I am crouched, holding the legs of

the wooden horse. Dad is the sandman. I am tired and my eyes and mouth are filled with sawdust. How long have I been asleep, tired, and numb? How many times have I swallowed the little white pills and forgotten everything? Dad stops sawing to hand me his handkerchief. I wipe my eyes, my cheeks, my mouth.

"Okay now, Emily?" Clutching the handsaw, Dad stretches his arms up to the sky. Then he shrinks back down to almost regular size. Gripping the top of the wooden horse again, he says, "I need you to hold this as steady as you can."

My throat scratches, and something inside of me is tickling like feathers stirring up through me, like a bird I've been keeping down there. A keeping bird. *Stay down there.* I stuff the handkerchief into my mouth and crouch down again to hold on to the legs of the horse, while Dad keeps sawing, whistling. *Chuck, chuck.*

The lines across Dad's forehead are etched into a deep frown. Then the end of the pole splits off and falls to the ground with a thud. Dad stops whistling, running his hands down his new mast. The horse stops moving. The sawdust is still. He wipes the beads of sweat from his face with his forearm, then swings the mast up onto his shoulder and carries it over to the hole John has dug to plant it in. I spit out his handkerchief and trail behind him. Dad turns and smiles at me. I step closer, my eyes sweeping the sky for a sign.

"Hold it like this. That's the way. That's the good kid," he says, smiling at me as I circle the post with both hands. He fills the dirt in around the pole, kicking it with his shoe, then using the back of his shovel to pat down the dirt. He stands back to admire his work. I know I'm finished, I can go. I turn and run to where they are.

All I smell is fish. With a fist, Mum crushes Ritz crackers in a plastic bag. She fingers soft butter and lemon juice through the crumbs and sprinkles in salt and pepper. I want to forget about what I saw, about her face and her hands, reaching up to grasp on to something. But her face is my face and Elizabeth Ruth's and Sarah's and Hope's. Pulling the scrod out on its broiler tray, Mum spreads the crumb mixture on top of the fish, then pushes the rack back in and shuts the oven door.

"John, Hope, Sarah, Elizabeth Ruth," Elizabeth Ruth says, putting a fork at each of our places. Bringing a fork to her mouth like a microphone, she sings with an awful twang, her eyes closed and one hand stretched over her heart, "I fall to pieces every time I see you. How could I be just your friend? I fall to pieces —"

"You're messing it up, Elizabeth Ruth," Hope says, and blocks her ears when Elizabeth Ruth repeats the same "I fall to pieces" line over and over as if that will make her heart more broken. Bowing, Elizabeth Ruth says to her absent audience, "Thank you very much, ladies and gentlemen." She returns to setting the table, adding, "One day I'm going to be famous. I'm going to sing like Patsy Cline."

"Elizabeth Ruth, what on earth did you do to yourself?" Mum asks, drying her hands on her apron. She marches over, shakes her head as she runs her fingers over Elizabeth Ruth's hairless hands, arms, neck, and face. "I don't know why you had to do that to your beautiful skin."

With a little sideways smile, Elizabeth Ruth shrugs back, and we all laugh at her. Mum shakes her head and says, "I don't know what I'm going to do with you."

All I want to do is be here surrounded by the steam of the corn boiling, the heat of the stove, the smell of warm rolls in the oven, the sound of water from the faucet, and all of us laughing.

I belong here.

Humming, Mum spreads herself all over the kitchen, pushing a pie crust flat, pressing it with the rolling pin, lifting flour, pushing to the right, then the left, the right, then the left. I squeeze my lips together to keep anything from coming out.

The flour has turned Mum's hands and arms and her chin and cheeks white. She gives me the blueberries and sugar and nutmeg to stir in a mixing bowl for the pie. I mix it all around and around, the whole time feeling like someone is watching me. A cloud passes by the window over the sink.

"How's the invention look?"

"Looks like a regular old sail to me."

We all crowd up against the window to see the sail flapping around Dad.

"That's it?"

"Well, it must do something," Mum says.

"Like what?"

"I don't know. Something."

When we go to tell Dad supper is ready, he says to us, "What do you think, kids? It's a highly sensitive flag and sail system that reflects the moon's light. It will be like sailing by sunlight, only better. She's a beauty. Smooth as silk."

A sail and an American flag, both with plastic reflecting sheaths, are rigged up to the pole I helped him cut. "We'll try her out tonight when it gets dark. This is it," he says, watching his flag and sail wave and flap in the breeze. "Yup, you bet."

"Time for supper, Dad." Sarah steps closer, "What makes it glitter so much? What's in the sheath to make it reflect the moonlight?"

He puts his hand up. "Whoa — that's close enough. I don't want anything to happen to her and you never know who's around the corner listening." He steps back to get a better view, with both hands on his hips, balancing his tall drink on his right side.

Sarah's hair swings side to side as we walk back to the kitchen. She points over to where the moon is becoming visible through the late afternoon sky and adds, "Look, it's only a half moon. I wonder if it'll be enough light for his great new invention. From the way he acts, you'd think he just walked on the moon or something." We eye each other about to laugh, but instead, sniffing the fishy supper smell, we plug our noses.

Mum uses a fork to press the top crust onto the bottom crust around the edge of her pie. Then she carefully stabs the top center into a star of holes and sprinkles it over lightly with sugar. Her dark eyes sparkle brighter than Dad's reflecting sheath as she takes hold of either side of my face and kisses me. "How's my Emily?" she asks.

I *am* her Emily.

I can feel the words rise in my throat. The pressure in my throat makes my mouth open and close, breath passing in and out. All of a sudden I want to tell Ham everything that has happened. Where are you, Ham? I know you're here somewhere.

As she bends to slide the pie in the oven, the outline of Mum's back ripples through her white cotton blouse. There's a photo of her posing in a black swimsuit, showing her swimmer's back. Her head dipped back, laughing, she's standing on a rock with one knee forward, an elbow bent, and her hand resting on her turned waist. Even though Mum doesn't swim much now, she still has a swimmer's back.

Mum holds up the baked scrod, all crispy brown on the outside, checking to see if it's cooked through the way Dad likes it. "Did you tell your father it's time for supper, Sarah?" she asks.

"Am I right or am I right?" Hope mimics Dad, putting her hands on her hips and clanking around the kitchen in a dizzy circle. She reaches up toward the top cabinet for one of Dad's whiskey bottles, slurring, "Let's see, I could get this if I weren't so drunk already." All of us, including Mum, are laughing, keeping an eye on the kitchen door.

"I told him," Sarah finally answers. "But I don't know if he'll be able to step away from his reflecting sail. Someone might try to steal it while he's not looking."

"Is that why you married him?" Hope asks. "Because you knew he'd be such a genius?"

When Hope lifts the top of the pot, her face disappears in steam. She plucks out the corn one by one, letting them drip before she stacks them up on a large plate.

The church bells slowly ring, telling us it's six o'clock. Outside the window we see Dad gazing up at his sail and flag. Mum looks down, puckering her bottom lip over the top, smiling and not smiling. "He never really had a father, you know. Pop died when he was so young."

Mum rubs the stubs of the missing fingertips on her small hand along the stove's edge, around the gas knobs. Skimming our eyes to see if we're still expecting an answer, she scoops the hot rolls into baskets lined with linen cloths.

"Well, he was so good-looking," she answers slowly. "After we were married I thought we'd share all our secrets." The idea of sharing secrets with Dad is so crazy that we all start giggling at once.

"Were you insane?" Elizabeth Ruth blurts out.

When Mum smiles, we do too, and then we all start laughing again. We can't help it, we can't stop. Somewhere outside a seagull's scream cuts through the air, a car skids to a stop, someone yells. Outside seems a million miles away. In here it's just us.

The screen door slaps shut. "What's so funny?" Luke asks, pinching his nose so his freckles disappear.

My sides ache. There's another buffalo nickel by Luke's feet. It's there and Luke doesn't even pick it up. That's why Luke's been talking to him and I keep finding buffalo nickels. I wonder if it's the same one, which would mean I have a hole in my pocket. It's cold in my pocket. Something is pushing through me. Ham is coming back.

"Everything's getting cold. Sit down in your places, everyone." Mum sweeps Owen into her arms, swirling the bottom of her wraparound skirt around her knees. "Youu-whoo," she calls Dad and John, "time for supper." Dad's invented something as big as the Magic Rose and Mum's like her old self again because everything's going to change now that Ham's coming back. She lights the new wicks of the tall white candles on either end of the table, which is much smaller than our long table in Cawood. Even without Ham here, we seem closer together, squishier, probably because everyone's grown since last year. Everyone, except me.

I keep waiting to grow, but every morning, I'm the same size, even though I spent every recess at St. Mary's hanging by my knees on the jungle gym to make myself longer. Ham had just started growing taller than me. I wonder if he's grown.

"I think it's a keeper," Dad tells Mum as he swaggers in. He pats Mum's head on his way to the kitchen sink, where he leans over, splashing the faucet water all over his face. He dries off with a dish towel and then pulls out his chair and sits down, placing his bottle of Tums beside his plate.

"I was looking at some of the houses up-island with the kids," he says. "We'll see." He immediately begins to chew his way through an ear of corn, sounding like an old hog. I wonder when they're going to tell me about Ham. I can't eat. I don't remember eating anything today.

"If everything goes right, I'm going to get a patent made for this one."

"That's going to be expensive." Mum puts the forkful of green beans back down on her plate.

Dad keeps chomping through the corn row by row, his face almost on top of his plate.

"There are still hospital bills," Mum says.

Dad doesn't answer her.

My brothers and sisters look at me. A breeze blows across the table, making the flames flicker and shine even brighter. A moth lands on top of the sunflowers, then flaps its wings, lingering there before it floats back up toward the ceiling. Ham's hospital bills haven't been paid. Everyone knows that. Has he been there this whole time? Is that what they're trying to tell me?

"Maybelle, Maybelle, elbows off the table." Hope breaks the silence.

"Maybelle, Maybelle yourself," Luke answers with his elbows sprawled out on either side of his plate.

"Luke," Mum says, "you know the rule. Elbows off the table." She lifts her nose in the air then automatically rises to reach into the oven for more hot rolls.

"Who wants a drop more fish?" She circles the table, carrying the pan of scrod, using her good hand to scoop with a large silver spoon.

As she bends herself over his plate, Dad stares at her hand still holding the serving spoon. "What's this?" he calls out, pulling her hand closer to him. She can't balance the pan, and the scrod covered in special crumb topping tips over and smashes onto the linoleum floor. Dad jumps to his feet without letting go of Mum's hand. All of a sudden, he takes up the whole kitchen.

"What happened to the goddamn diamond?" he demands. He shakes her hand furiously, bending it back and forth at the wrist.

We stare at Mum's hand without the diamond. Luke slips his elbows off the table, pulling his arms down by his sides. I shrink into my seat, hiding my hands between my legs, pressing there, squeezing hard, thinking, *Please don't hurt her.*

"Where is the diamond?" he demands, even louder. He throws her hand into the light of the window. The air is buzzing. I squeeze myself so tight, I can barely breathe.

"It must have fallen out," Mum says, beside him. "It has to be around here somewhere. We'll find it. I know we will." She pulls her ring finger close to her and wraps her small hand tight around it.

Dad smiles, his mouth flashing like a revolving door. He fixes himself a tall glass of Jameson whisky, clinking the ice, grabs a couple slices of white bread, and opens the kitchen door, letting it slap on the toe of his shoe. "Tomorrow we'll all go to Sunday mass," he tells us, and then he is gone.

I let go of myself. Ham is gone.

"Now he wants to go to church," Hope blurts out, "after we haven't gone since the funeral."

Oh, that's where Ham is, I realize.

Out of the corner of my eye, I see Mum's hand snatch up Dad's empty glass of milk and hurl it at the wall beside the door where the washing machine is tucked into the corner. The glass shatters like thousands of diamonds everywhere.

"That's better," she says to us. She doesn't bother to pick up the glass or the baked scrod spilled all over the floor. She pulls out a gallon of Hood vanilla ice cream from the freezer and heats her fudge sauce in a pan on the stove. Mum stands by the oven with her hands on her hips, elbows out, looking over us, her gaze holding us all together here, telling us everything will work out.

"I don't know who he thinks he is," she says, shaking her head toward Dad. We can see him through the window, standing on the lawn, holding a slice of white bread in one hand and, in the other, his glass. I wonder if he can see himself smiling on the shiny reflecting sheath, flapping in the breeze as the sun goes down.

"We don't have to finish supper first?" Luke asks, amazed.

"Not tonight," Mum says. "Supper's over."

"Cool," John says.

Owen starts crying from his crib, so Hope scoops the ice

cream into dishes for us. There Dad is and here we are, eating ice cream sundaes while our supper lies on the table and all over the floor. There are no rules anymore. Everything has snapped.

"Meeting in the shed after the dishes," Hope whispers to me. I am drying the dishes Hope washes and Sarah puts away. Elizabeth Ruth is sweeping the floor. John pries the top off Dad's Tums and pops a bunch of them into his mouth.

"That's disgusting," Hope tells him.

"They're good. They taste like Sweetarts," he tells her.

"Let me taste one," she says, snatching a few from his hands. "Hmm, these are good. Try one." She gives us each one. Mine is sweet orange. We eat them all.

"Better get rid of the bottle," Hope tells John. He disappears.

We sneak out to the shed as quietly as we can so Dad doesn't see us. The crickets are so loud it seems like some of them have landed in my brain.

"There she goes, Bud, lighting up the sky like a goddamn beacon," Dad says. His reflecting sail and flag are glowing under the moonlight, flapping around in the wind. The light spreads around Dad as if he were a huge firefly. Dad tilts his head back and cries out to Bud, "Thatta boy."

"What an idiot," Hope says once we are safe in the shed. Behind her the long sunflowers are bending their fat heads down, blowing back and forth, making shadows run across the window.

There is a knock on the door. "Can I come in?" John asks, walking in. The burned bramble sounds like newspaper crinkling in the wind.

"Do we have a choice?" Hope returns.

"I have a surprise," he says. His eyes have a wild look as he pulls Dad's whiskey bottle out from under his shirt.

"He's going to find out if we drink it," Sarah says immediately.

"Not if we mark it and fill what we drank with water. And

it's not like it's the only bottle in the house." He unscrews the top, wagging it beneath his nose, then tips the bottle back into his mouth, grimacing, shaking his head. He passes the bottle to Hope, who sits down and does the same, wiping her mouth with the back of her hand. We crouch down around Hope. Sarah takes the bottle. A small sip makes her eyes water. Hope and John laugh at her, but I don't. Elizabeth Ruth drinks fast, pulling the bottle back and laughing as she squeezes and shakes her face. When I look at her, I only see Elizabeth Ruth. I'm glad I'm not her.

It's my turn. Everybody is waiting. The bottle is smooth and heavy in my hand. The burning liquor passes through my mouth, making my throat go hot. I want to throw it all up before it can get down. But once it's down there, it spreads across my chest, warming me.

The bottle goes back to John. "Let's look outside," he says, rocking on his heels.

We all look out toward the sail, but the moon has gone under a cloud, and though we know the flag is there, we can barely see the shape of it moving in and out of the darkening night. It's there, then it's not there. Dad keeps standing there with Bud sniffing around him. We laugh at them watching the reflecting sail go dim in the empty night, then sit down again in our circle, passing Dad's bottle.

"I guess it's not going to be the next big one," Sarah says. We all start laughing and we can't stop. I know I'll see him tomorrow, but I keep seeing Ham in their eyes, their mouths, their hands as the room spins around.

When do I get to see Ham? I ask them. *Tell me.*

The bottle goes around again. They can't hear me.

I'm trying to keep the floor from turning upside down when Hope pulls the wooden box that used to be in Dad's closet out from underneath her cot. She sets it in the center of our circle and says, fingering the brass padlock, "Who wants to see what's in here?"

"You stole that?" John says, taking another sip of whiskey.

"No, I borrowed it so I could see what's inside," Hope answers.

"What's it sound like?"

"Nothing," Hope says, shaking the box. "I think it's a letter. Or maybe a will."

"Maybe you'll inherit the Tiger Soap," John tells her.

"Better than the woodstove," she answers.

"Elizabeth Ruth'll get the chickens," John says.

"I'll take the Tums." Sarah laughs.

"What'll Emily get?" Elizabeth Ruth asks.

"She'll get her voice back." Hope pauses. They don't know what else to do, so they laugh.

"Open it, then," John tells her. Hope turns the box upside down.

"Youu-whoo." Mum calls from the house for me to get ready for bed.

"Oh great," Sarah says. "What if she comes out here? Then what do we do?"

"Don't worry," John says. He takes a tube of Colgate from the back pocket of his jeans.

Outside, music suddenly smashes its way out of the car over to us, in huge waves, swelling, then falling, smashing like the glass Mum threw against the wall. Dad is sitting in the Oldsmobile with the door wide open, music pouring out.

"What's he doing?" Elizabeth Ruth asks.

"Everyone's going to complain," Sarah adds, sucking the toothpaste straight from the tube.

"It's Beethoven," Hope says.

In the thunder of music, nobody dares to move. Everything seems to be held in the force of the symphony cutting through the air, billowing up to the sky and then slipping back and collapsing. The fog pushes across the sky and covers the moon completely. Beethoven replaces the light that has disappeared.

"What's going on out there?" someone yells.

"Turn it down, would you?" another neighbor yells.

Mum steps out into the dark, clutching the open back of her johnny. All of us, even Mum, wear the johnnies Dad took from the hospital as nightgowns, but not outside! She makes her way carefully on the edges of her bare feet over the small stones and shells covering the driveway, to the Oldsmobile. Her hair hangs wet and uneven at her shoulders. When she gets to the car, we can see that she has covered her face with a layer of ointment like she does every night before bed. Glowing, Mum reaches her small hand to her shining throat.

Then the music stops as simply as it started and he unrolls the window and reaches his hand out toward her. Don't let him hurt you this time, Mum, I am about to yell to her, my voice thumping inside of me.

Mum is a streak of white running back to the house. She doesn't hold the split down the back of her johnny closed, and she doesn't walk carefully on the sides of her feet. She runs and the sides of her johnny flap open, like the sail slapping through the night air.

Seconds later she is walking fast, her right arm stretched carefully out in front of her, holding his tall glass full and clinking. Mum carries Dad's drink to him in the night. No one says a word, but it seems like the game we were playing is over.

When I am ready for bed, Mum comes into my room. Her face looks as if it is being pulled by strings. Sitting on the edge of my bed, she blesses me, my eyes, my ears, nose, and mouth. She blesses everyone in the family from oldest to youngest. Then she stops and, squeezing her hands together, glances around the room as if she's trying to find something else to bless.

Mum's face glows like the reflecting flag is supposed to. She glides her hands over her cheeks, down to her chin and up across her forehead, under and around her eyes, spreading the ointment evenly across her skin. Outside the car door slams, the sound echoing into the stillness that follows. I bet she's wondering, like I am, where he's going and what he's doing.

Mum doesn't know I can't sleep because I don't want anything to happen to her. She's too far away. As quickly as she shuts off the light, closes the door, and is gone, I try to make her everywhere, blessing me again, saying I am hers, but all I hear is the screen door slapping open and closed and a tin shrill whistling.

Where are you, Ham? There is no light from the moon but the streetlamp on the corner casts enough light to make shadows in the darkest corners of the room. Since I cannot close my eyes, I watch the shadows grow huge and press against me. I think if I don't move or make a sound, they won't be able to tell I'm here. If I concentrate hard enough, I can turn my whole self into a single ear on the pillow.

I remember Elizabeth Ruth's song — *When the sun goes down, the sandman comes, to sprinkle sand in the eyes of his little ones* — as the shapes in here roll in and out like the waves on the shore, sucking under, rolling back, and disappearing again.

These shadows want me to be one of them, to come closer, into the corners of the room with them. *I am an ear,* I tell myself, a single ear resting on the pillow. I hold my breath as long as I can so they'll forget I'm here. Slowly as possible, so I don't make a ripple in the bedcovers, I drag my hand like a smooth stone up along my thigh, over my private, to my stomach. I have disappeared. I am only an ear. I drag my hand up to where my heart is beating so loudly. I press it there to hold the banging inside my chest before they hear me. I'm going to burst.

Ham, when are you coming back?

From the kitchen comes the sound of running water. It runs

through the pipes, then it stops and the screen door slams again. I don't know how long I lie there, but I know time is passing because that was one second and now it is gone. I stop counting the seconds when I hear something barking outside, soft and sharp. It sounds like the way it does on TV when the noise comes from somewhere beyond the dog, not from the dog's mouth. The fog slips across the yard, and the wind is a shrill whistle cutting through the dark shapes. I pull the covers off in a single sweep and run for the light switch. In the brightness, everything is just like it was.

I don't make a sound opening the door. The wooden floor is cold beneath my bare feet as I follow the light and the smell coming from the kitchen. The faint then harsh barking is becoming clearer now. It must be Ham calling. *Woof, woof! That's a good dog, Ham.* The barking is all I can make out through the thick air. Scared to death, I walk toward it. I can't feel anything as I follow the sound that will finally take me to Ham. Finally. I have been waiting so long, keeping myself for him.

The ground is wet with dew and the sky covered by clouds, making the world seem to cave in on me. Behind me a foghorn begins blowing as steadily as my heart beating and I feel like I am being pulled into a dark tunnel. I cannot help myself, can't stop myself anymore. Afraid of what will be at the end, I want the air to stop pulling me there. I want to lie down in the fog and wet grass and stay there.

There is the dog with a long hard nose, crooked teeth, and eyes of blue water shining through the dark. Beside the window of the shed where my sisters are, the dog is barking, I hear barking. He's the only thing I see. *Here I am, Ham. It's Emily,* I am about to say when the dog starts toward me.

Something is wrong, his mouth is open, ready to bite. The nose is too long for a dog's and the eyes are icy blue circles rolling inside the mask. They are coming toward me, dark and fierce, like bullets, like madness. The dog stares at me with an unmoving face and laughs like Dad laughs. It's not Ham. It's only a mask, it's the painted dog mask that Ham made for Dad.

I think I am going to die when the huge dog stumbles forward, grabbing me around the wrist. What are you going to do to me, Dad? Am I going to die like Ham did?

I see his shadow moving behind Ham at the bridge. I jumped when you said three, Dad. I jumped, then I saw him falling in a twisted heap into the sea. You made him jump. *You pushed him.* Dad.

Dad's thick fingers tighten around my wrist. I can see his hand, the picture of it flashes through my brain. You pushed him, Dad. *Ham, where are you?* Dad's hands are strangling my wrists, my arms, my neck, everything, digging his fingernails deeper into the soft underside of my skin, my veins. This time I have to do something.

I scream from so far down, it feels like I'm cracking, splitting in half. This dog can't reach his hand around to cover my mouth and it's too late anyway. I'm screaming, screaming out everything.

Listen to me, Ham. Can you hear me?

The clouds break a passageway through the sky, uncovering the half moon, then it is gone again. Dad stands quietly by his reflecting sail, flapping in the wind. My sisters are beside me.

"Can you hear me?" I whisper, forcing the words out. It's easy.

"Of course," Hope says. "I think the whole island heard you."

"Emily?" Sarah and Elizabeth Ruth say at the same time. They look at each other and call to Mum who's walking across the lawn to us.

"Hurry, Mum," they tell her. "Emily can talk again."

Mum is saying my name out loud over and over. Dad has disappeared. I can talk.

Mrs. Jenkins turns her lights on across the street and steps out onto her porch. "Anything I can do?"

I have been heard! Here I am, Emily Stone, loud enough to wake the neighbors.

"Everything's fine, thank you," Mum calls over to Mrs. Jenkins. Other neighbors are waiting on their porches, too, to find out about whatever woke them so late at night.

"Everything all right?" Mr. Brillhart calls over. He puts a match to the bowl of his pipe, then waves it out.

Mum bunches her hair into a ponytail with her fingers, then pulls the back of her hospital johnny closed. "We're fine, thank you. A sleepwalker, that's all," she lies and then starts backing up toward the kitchen door, and we all follow her.

John and Luke are standing barefoot on the "Home Is Where the Heart Is" doormat. "What happened?" Luke asks.

"Emily can talk again," Elizabeth Ruth blurts out.

"Say something," Luke tells me.

"Something," I say.

"She can!" He sounds surprised. "Say something else."

Mum takes the gallon of milk from the refrigerator, pours it into a saucepan on the stove, and adds sugar and cocoa. Everyone stares at me, waiting for me to start talking, but I'm just getting used to my mouth again, my tongue sweeping around in there like a feather. I'm rolling my tongue on the roof of my mouth and all over and around my gums. It's warm in there. I don't want to run out of air to breathe so I'm saving my breath — not holding it, just saving it.

"When are you going to talk?" Luke wants to know.

"Why did you stop talking for so long?" John asks.

"Yeah, what happened, Emily?" Elizabeth Ruth asks. They wait for me to say something.

Something is pushing around inside my mouth, but I don't

want to say what I saw. I don't know what to tell them. I had to stop talking. Ham stopped talking.

There is a clanging sound outside the window, of metal hitting metal, cutting through the quiet as Dad slams the lid down on the trash can. "Fuck, fuck, fuck," he says in the rhythm of the slamming. Each time he says it, the blood rushes across my face.

No one moves. We watch each other, waiting for him to stop, and he does. Mum doesn't say she is afraid of his icy eyes or his iron face. She doesn't ask us what we should do. She stands at the stove, stirring the chocolate milk.

"I wish we could go somewhere new, like Florida, and start all over. And I wish he didn't have to come with us," Hope finally says, sighing.

"For heaven's sake, Hope," Mum says quickly, "we're not going to have any more trouble tonight."

"Well, it's true," Hope tells her. "And what was he doing out there tonight anyway?"

Mum's eyes are breaking away, escaping off her face, then they are there in front of us, telling us all that she knows. Her face is full of light and shadows, rising and falling with her quick breaths. "I don't know why he wears that foolish thing. He does the best he can. And that's all he can do," she says, tucking her lips tight inside her mouth. "He doesn't mean to hurt anyone."

"Oh, no," Hope says softly.

"What does he wear every night?" Elizabeth Ruth asks.

"What does he wear, Mum?" they ask her.

Mum's eyes are sharp and wet. She doesn't say anything about the dog mask Ham made for Dad on Father's Day.

I see Dad wearing his dog mask, hiding in the shadows of every corner of the room, loafing and spying through the windows. Dad is watching us with a tight eye, blowing his whistle, kicking Luke, saying fuck, fuck, fuck. I wonder what he would have done if I hadn't yelled so loud and if he hadn't stumbled. I thought he was going to kill me.

I blow the small bubbles from the middle of my chocolate milk to the outer edges, trying to see myself in my drink. I can't wait anymore. In one rush of breath, I ask, "Where is Ham?"

A funny noise escapes out of Mum's mouth. Dropping her eyes, Sarah chokes on her hot chocolate. The others look at me like I'm crazy. Someone giggles nervously.

"Doesn't she know he's dead?" Luke whispers.

Mum tilts her head to the side, her eyes settling, her lips softening again. She catches herself, composes herself just as the Oldsmobile door slams outside.

The screen door creaks, stretching slowly open, and there is Dad. Where's your mask, Dogface? His eyes are blue pellets penetrating into all of us. I can't look. Stay out of sight, I tell myself, reaching my hand up over my eyes so I can't see him.

"Time for bed, everyone. Don't forget, we're all going to the ten o'clock mass tomorrow." Mum's voice cracks. She blasts the faucet on, filling up the empty saucepan with the hot water and soap.

We file over to Mum to kiss her good night. I lift my hand like a blinder over my eyes for a second to touch my lips to hers. I won't look at Dad, and I won't kiss him either. Hope does, and Sarah and Elizabeth do, too, but I can't — not even when he puts his cold face close to mine.

"It wasn't my fault," I whisper, my eyes blocked from him, holding me there by the elbow, waiting for me to kiss him good night.

"What?" he calls out. "What'd you say to me?"

I'm afraid when I uncover my eyes in the absolute quiet.

"Who do you think you are?" he yells out at me, throwing his hands up, sliding himself forward.

I think I am Emily Stone. It's not exactly his hand or foot striking me that I run away from. It's all the blood rushing into my face, like I'm dissolving. Except that now I have my new voice and he can't touch me there, that's what I'm thinking as I fall on my face on the wet grass on the lawn outside the kitchen door. I laugh to myself — what else can I do? I'll never be who he wants me to be.

In the thin light of the half moon, I see Dad with his shirt hanging out of his loose pants, like a bandaged bomb, unraveling, unwrapping. Because I'm talking. Hope reaches her hand toward me, mumbling that she'd like to kill him.

8

Hope leads me back into the shed, where she kicks the door falling off its hinges upright into the corner. It creaks and thuds, chipping faded paint. She drags the middle cot over, propping it against the door to keep anyone from coming in. They're waiting for me to talk. The sunflowers outside the window have drooped their big heads and folded over each other, while the crickets are chirping and the swallows singing in the early morning. There's no one keeping us in order anymore. Only us. Something has snapped.

"Ham's never coming back, is he?" I ask them.

"No, he's buried," Hope says, her arms folded across her chest. "You were there, don't you remember?"

I saw a bluebird high up in the tree, but I never saw him. Past them, the half moon is dipping and dissolving into the clouds through the window where Hope stands. *He's never coming back.*

"We thought you knew," Sarah says, nodding.

I need to hold on to something before I collapse. Nothing

makes sense. There's no reason to talk now, I'm not ever going to talk again. I suck in my breath and wait for the white sheet to fall in front of my face, to cover everything. The faces of my sisters begin to blur into whiteness.

"You still have him, Emily," Sarah says. "Everything you remember about him." As soon as she puts her hand on my head, running her fingers through my hair, the outline of her becomes clear. She is right there in front of me. I take a breath.

"Why don't you talk to us, Emily?" Elizabeth Ruth asks, crouched in front of me.

I take another gulp of air.

"Say something. Tell us what you want to say," Hope says.

My voice seems to be outside of me now, flying crazily around the room, waiting to land. I have to say it. "I didn't want Ham to die," I finally manage to say. It wasn't my fault, I tell myself.

They come closer.

"Nobody did, Emily. We thought that's why you stopped talking. Because he died," Hope says. They look at each other, confused.

"What else happened, Emily? What happened at the bridge?"

"Why'd you stop talking?"

How do I tell them everything? The words press through me and through the darkness that is covering me. I have to tell them. "He didn't want to jump." They're waiting.

"What do you mean?"

"He tried to turn and grab onto the bridge and hit his chin."

"Did you see it?"

They wait for me to say more. It all happens again. Right as I jumped, Dad's quick shadow was behind me and then I fell into the shadows of the sea. Ham is turning and twisted all wrong, a hole in his chin bleeding. And the camera is hanging around Dad's neck. Dad wanted to take a picture of us jumping together with his new Instamatic. He'd just bought it. I feel an enormous weight sink through me, and the words fly out of me, "Dad made him. He wanted a picture of us jumping."

"Oh," Sarah gasps.

"A photo?" Hope asks.

"He wanted to take a photo?" Elizabeth Ruth repeats.

"I can't believe it. I don't know why Mum doesn't ever do anything. I hate him." Hope rises, her eyes fierce and her mouth hard. "I can't stand him anymore. I wish *he* were dead. It'd be so much better without him."

The whole world is speeding past us and we are the only thing staying in one place. How can I go inside the house again? How can Mum stay in there? My world is collapsing. How will it ever get right again?

"I could fix the brake pedal so he'd smash up the next time he takes out the Oldsmobile." Hope's words sound so strangely horrible, we can't help but laugh out loud.

"Well, what else could we do? Loosen a tire?" she asks. "It'd probably fall off in the driveway."

"Remember when Mum almost crashed on the highway because the steering alignment, or something, was off? You could do that," Elizabeth Ruth suggests, excited, folding her hairless legs into a pretzel, leaning closer to us.

"*You* could do that," Hope tells her. "Or what if we threw him a rag lit on fire while he was underneath the car fixing something?" Her pale face glows in the flame of the match she touches to the wick of a candle.

"Oh, disgusting," Sarah says, giggling. "If we were smart, we'd do something like poison him, but that'd take too long."

"Or we could go sightseeing up-island and push him off the Gay Head cliffs." Elizabeth Ruth cranes her neck back and laughs hysterically like she can't believe what she said. We all laugh, because we have snapped. We are making him nothing and ourselves everything. There is no order.

"I can't believe she actually married him," Elizabeth Ruth says, switching on Hope's portable radio.

I hear bits of the song over the static. "When tears come down —" His voice is soft and gruff like he's got something in there.

"And stays married to him. I'd never marry anyone like that. No way," Hope says, turning away from us to write her name with her finger through the dust on the windowpane.

I try to listen to the man singing about his cheating heart. "You'll cry and cry and try —"

"You know what she said? That she made a promise to God," Hope continues. "God's not that stupid — He'd change His mind, but she'll stay with *Dad* forever."

"Your cheatin' heart —" I wish Hope would stop talking so I could hear the radio, "— will tell on you."

"I still can't believe it," Sarah says.

"Did you see the camera?"

I nod.

"I wish we could move to Florida. It's so warm and there are oranges growing everywhere. You can just pick them right off the tree and eat them whenever you want," Elizabeth Ruth says, halfclosing her eyes. "That's what Grandma said."

My head is spinning and I know I have to go to bed. I wish I could sleep out here, but I have to go inside with him. I can't make sense of anything anymore. Hope helps me haul the cot away from where it blocks the shed door.

While my eyes get used to the darkness, I follow the gleam of the metal trash cans lined up outside the kitchen. I am sliding past them when I spot Ham's dog mask lying broken beneath one of the lids. I pull the mask out by the elastic. Its papier-mâché ears are pointed like a wolf's and cracked at the tips, and its mouth is open like a saw cutting the night. I let its two uneven holes for eyes sway away from me, seeing Dad behind them.

At first I think Elizabeth Ruth is playing Hope's radio louder, but then I realize the music is coming from the Oldsmobile. Dad's right arm rests over the roof with the front door wide open and one foot in the car as he stares up at his reflecting flag, flapping against itself, not reflecting anything. Quiet waves of classical music seep out, pounding, then seeping again. He seems so small and worn-out.

I try to picture Dad in bed with the mask on. I can't figure out where he kept it all this time. The holes cut out of the mask for eyes swing around in the dark, like black marbles disappearing, then gleaming at me. They are watching me like they know everything, like they knew Ham was never coming back all along.

"Throw it away!" Hope whispers sharply, sucking air as she steps out of the dark without any warning. "Go ahead. It's bad luck."

I shove it down beneath the layers of corn silk and husks, through the stems of green beans, a milk jug, fishy-smelling Glad cling wrap, the Ritz cracker box, burying the mask in all today's garbage.

"Good-bye," I say under my breath and place the lid back on top of the trash can. As soon as Hope sees this, she turns to go to the shed. Before he sees me, I run inside.

Mum is standing over me in bed, telling me, "That's my good girl. I'm so glad you're talking again, Emily. I knew you would. I've been praying for you every day. Tomorrow, we'll have a little party to celebrate." She places her hand on my forehead. "You feel hot. Do you feel all right, Emily?"

"Where is Ham, Mum?"

"He's in heaven now," she tells me quickly. "You know that."

I have to see if the buffalo nickels are still in the pockets of my shorts.

"You look pale," she says. "Did you eat enough today? How about an ice cream? Do you want an ice cream, Emily?"

I say, "I want an orange. Why can't we go to Florida?"

"Florida?" Her hand covers my forehead. "I think you have a fever."

"There are oranges you can pick right off the trees, the kind that peel in one whole piece."

"Shhh, go to sleep now," she says. "Nobody's going anywhere. Go to sleep now. Everything's going to be fine in the morning." Mum's heat circles me and I know at least she'll never leave me. I go to sleep and dream I'm wearing a fluffy white dress. It's so fluffy that I am like a balloon bobbing over everyone, including Ham. Ham is there in my dream. I wave to him.

The sun pouring through the windows wakes me, telling me to remember something. Something has changed. I am different somehow. I am alone. I want to be back in my dream, but then I remember today is the party for me. Mum is padding through the kitchen, where the others talk in low voices. Everything that happened last night comes back in one big sweep of pictures. I have to talk again.

"Good morning," I say out loud to myself. I practice again, louder, then softer. I stretch my lips to say it in a deep voice like Dad, then like Elizabeth Ruth doing Patsy Cline. I swing myself out of bed, pulling myself toward the light. "Good morning, good morning, good morning." It's too hard. I don't want to talk. I wish I could just go back to how I was — when I thought Ham was coming back.

I peek into the kitchen. Everyone is watching Mum soak slices of bread in her cream-and-egg batter and sprinkle them with cinnamon. She wipes her hands on her flowered apron and flips

the bread over, soaking the other side before she lifts the dripping bread onto the grill.

In his carriage pulled up to the table, Owen is opening and
closing his mouth. Luke closes his mouth over Owen's fist. "All
gone," he says, and then, when he lets Owen's wet hand out of his
mouth, he shouts, "There it is. There's Owen's hand." Owen
stares around the table. I wish I were him.

"Good morning," I announce shakily.

"Told you," Luke says, poking Elizabeth Ruth in the side with
his fork.

"I didn't say she wouldn't talk at *all*," Elizabeth Ruth whispers
back.

"Morning, Emily," the others say back.

I hide myself in between them so they'll stop looking at me.

Hope pours our cups full of orange juice. Bacon sizzles and
spatters in the frying pan Mum sets on the cutting board. Mum
soaks another piece of bread in the batter, stopping to look out
the window every once in a while.

"Is he out there yet?" Elizabeth Ruth asks, then turns to me.
"The Oldsmobile and his stupid sail were gone this morning."

"And him."

Mum sighs. "I guess it didn't go so well." Her bun has come
loose, spreading strands of hair over her back like a dark fan.

"Did he tell you the secret of the reflecting sheath before he
took it away?" Hope asks.

"She can't tell us," John answers. "We might try to sell it to the
neighbors."

Mum doesn't say anything as she lifts the French toast off the
grill onto a plate. She's in here with us and she's out there wherever Dad is.

"Aren't you going to talk?" Luke asks me.

"Maybe," I answer, watching a large pat of butter melt over a
stack of French toast. Together the butter and cream smell like

Owen. When Luke gives Owen a crust of toast, he squishes it between his tiny fingers, then tries to suck it all in between his gums.

"He can't eat toast, you idiot," Hope says, prying out the soggy toast.

"Hope, it's Sunday. And, Luke, don't waste food when there are children starving in India," Mum says automatically.

"Why don't you send it to India, then?" John asks.

"There are children starving a lot closer than that," Hope says.

I hate all of them. Because they aren't Ham. They can't help it, but I still hate them. "Ham," I say. The maple syrup glistens on the fork frozen in front of Elizabeth Ruth's mouth. Hope clears her throat, Sarah stops making holes in her French toast and drops her eyes to her plate, and Luke looks at all of us like he doesn't know whether to laugh or not. Owen is just Owen.

Mum stands at the kitchen sink, scrubbing each plate and glass, fork, knife, and spoon until they're spotless, and scouring every inch of the sink, each corner, up along the neck of the faucet, carefully under the nozzle, around the base of the hose, her good hand moving in quick circles. Why are you cleaning and ordering everything all the time when nothing else makes sense? I want to ask her.

"It's almost time to get ready for church," Mum says to us, which means finish eating, get dressed, and go.

No one knows where Dad is or what happened to his reflecting flag and sail. With our hair combed neat and our best shoes on, we walk to church and find he's not in the polished pew we follow Mum into, either.

Mum closes her eyes, folds her hands in her lap, and lowers her head, breathing in and then out.

Gazing up the length of a column with white curls rolling out of the top, I imagine palm trees and orange trees on white sandy beaches under the open Florida sky. I am dreaming about picking oranges from the trees above and peeling them in one peel when the priest enters, spreading his willowy arms, lifting his tiny head, and telling us to rise. He was the priest at Ham's funeral. I hate him, too, and his tiny head. I don't even want to look at him.

I shiver through my dress, clutching myself, listening to Mum sing off tune. I block my ears and squint so tight, he becomes a speck, as small as the pointed yellow flowers on my stupid dress, which used to be Elizabeth Ruth's and before that Sarah's and Hope's. Eleven years is way too old for a dress like this with flowers all over it. It should go straight into the Goodwill box. I close my eyes and make the priest all covered in bloody wounds and brown scabs, mangled and dying like Jesus with a crown of thorns, dying on the cross. I don't know why they're all paying attention to him when he's the one who buried Ham. How could they want anything to do with him? When I raise my eyes to the altar, though, I discover this priest isn't the leper or the crucified Jesus I turned him into. His arms are open and he is smiling, his face as bright as the Jesus on the cover of our *Bible Stories for Children.*

Mum's face is like that, too — like Jesus' and the priest's — only Mum's is right there in front of me, full of soft yellow light. I wonder what this priest is saying and decide to inch my fingers out from deep inside my ears for a second. Except for people shuffling in the pews, it is quiet. His voice, strong and even, says, "Through the transformation of love, we, our children, and grandchildren will live freely, without the fear of war." I think he is only looking at me as he talks. "Jesus had a love this great, a brotherly, selfless love, big enough for everyone. It is the same love a mother has for her children."

He pauses, fixing his eyes on me again, then continues.

"Mother Teresa says she doesn't do great things. She does small things with great love. Let us all go out into the community and do small things with great love. As is each mother's love for her children, so is Jesus' love for all mankind. Mothers and fathers, do unto each other and do unto others as you would do unto your own children —"

Easy for him to say, I think. My face goes hot. He doesn't know anything about Dad. He doesn't know anything.

I turn to Sarah and whisper, "He's the one who buried Ham."

She lifts her eyes to mine. "What else was he supposed to do?"

I don't want to believe it. And I don't want it to be my fault. All I want is to be good. I want Jesus to forgive me for everything. I just want to be good like Mum. I want to have Mum's face. Jesus must know. Jesus, behind the altar, His face like Mum's, calls me closer. My body rises toward Him, He has called me. All the voices sing out at once, "And He will raise you up on eagles' wings." I don't hate them anymore and I'm not mad anymore. I don't really feel anything at all, like when Dad puts those white pills in my drink. Through the stained glass, I see the clouds dotting the sky.

Everyone leaves the church except for me and Mum. We stay in the pew with our heads bent in prayer. I slide back and forth on the slippery polished pew, looking from Mum's face to Jesus' face to her stubby small hands to Jesus' hands nailed into the cross. Everything He did is for us, isn't that right, Mum? Just like with you. I saw what happened, Mum. She did it for us. Her face is my face pressed down to the floor in the dark. My hand is her small hand. The thing is, I know this, but now it all makes sense, like it was the only way it could have happened, like it was someone else's decision.

Sitting in church with sunlight passing down through the stained glass onto me, I know, too, I have to suffer to get all the badness out. I want to get rid of my sins and be good like she is. I drop my head so my chin tucks into my chest and I pray to Jesus. I tell Him I'm not going to be bad anymore. It hurts, like something is sticking in my side. I'm going to change, I really am. When Mum nudges me, I slide to the end of the pew, where the stack of missals is, and rise.

As I walk through the sea grass by the lagoon toward the dock, my best shoes sink into the wet sand, soaking my feet through. I can still see Jesus perfectly. He is like a beautiful woman, with His long golden hair falling over the thin shoulders of His curved, naked body, only a strap of cloth over His private.

After the stations of the cross one Good Friday, Ham found two pieces of scrap wood in Dad's garage and nailed them together in a cross. Then he got Elizabeth Ruth's Barbie doll, bare naked except for her white bikini bottoms, and hammered her hands straight to the cross with Dad's sixpenny nails. From wearing such high heels, her feet wouldn't rest flat on the wood, one on top of the other, so Ham could nail only one foot to the cross.

The sun was just going down, surrounding us with a gray-blue mist that made Barbie seem to float when he propped her up against the juniper tree in our backyard. I thought she was so pretty with her blond hair neatly falling over her perky tips. And the way she was smiling pink and kicking out her free leg, Barbie didn't seem to mind being crucified at all.

Elizabeth Ruth minded, though. When she came around back to call us for supper and saw Barbie, she screamed. Not bothering to listen to Ham explain how it was just like Jesus' death, Elizabeth Ruth yanked Barbie off the cross and rolled her into her blouse. It was when she opened her shirt to check Barbie that she noticed the missing hand and splintered foot and screamed again, "How could you do this?"

"She wanted me to," Ham said, speaking for Barbie.

Elizabeth Ruth stamped her foot and spun off, cradling Barbie's head.

"Are you going to tell?" Ham asked, trotting after her. "Are you, Elizabeth Ruth?"

Swinging her skinny hips, she kept walking, carrying Barbie all the way to the kitchen. I knew she wouldn't tell Dad, because we would have all gotten in trouble. She only told Mum. Mum took one look and told Elizabeth Ruth to be thankful Barbie still had her arms and legs and, of course, Elizabeth Ruth had to start crying.

This morning I wanted Jesus to fill the inside of me so bad I thought I was going to cry. I didn't, though. I'm done with crying. Right then I know exactly what I have to do.

I squeeze Dad's metal razor tighter around my fingers in my palm. It's not as cold now as when I took it from where he left it gleaming silver on top of the bathroom sink. When I saw it had his dark stubs of whiskers caught in the space between the blade and the metal, I was going to search for a clean blade, but I didn't want anyone to find me. So without saying a word to my sisters in the shed or Mum in the kitchen, I sneaked through the back door with the razor.

Up ahead past the dock, a trail of gray clouds lines the edge of sky above the seawater. As I step over the stumps of marshy grass, that same song playing on Hope's radio last night keeps bumping through my head. It's funny that with all those church hymns fresh in my mind, the words that keep coming back to me are "Your cheatin' heart will tell on you."

I'm going to do it for Ham. I'm going to cut all that badness out for him.

I know why I've come here, I know what I have to do, but my whole body stops still and I almost drop the razor in the willows when I see the dock in front of me. I grab myself between the legs, but it's too late—a warm trickle runs down my legs, into my socks, into my best shoes. I'm turning inside out, I am leaking.

I walk up onto the dock, where I used to come all the time with Ham. It's how it always was. Seaweed and barnacles have dried unevenly on the posts on either side of the flat planks of the dock. The slow rolling water smells fishy as it laps toward me.

Something snaps behind me, and I turn quickly to skim my eyes across the marsh grass behind our house for Dad, but he's not there. It's the wind rustling and whispering through everything. He hasn't been home all night.

Something shines up ahead. It's another one of Dad's buffalo nickels. Sarah was right. Ham's still here somewhere because I keep finding him.

Ham stole the glass jar of buffalo nickels that Dad had been collecting for years, just like his father, from the top shelf in his closet next to the locked wooden box. When he realized they were missing, Dad called the police. "What the hell is so funny? Don't you know who this is?" We watched him stand there turning red, pulling the telephone cord straight across the kitchen.

"You want *me* to look for them?" He laughed.

"Isn't that your job?"

"Why don't you search your ass?" he finally shouted and hung up the telephone. Then he divided us up to search each other's rooms — a search party in our own house! Nobody found them.

I thought Ham used all the buffalo nickels to buy the expensive chocolates from the department store for Mum's birthday. No one asked where he got the money for them. We ate them all — the strawberry creams, raspberry creams, coconut fills, dark truffles — in the morning when Dad was working in the garage. Now I keep finding those buffalo nickels everywhere.

I slide the nickel into the pocket of my dress for good luck and spread myself belly-down on the edge of the dock, facing the water, pulling myself closer to the cooing and feathery sounds rising through the wood. There are swallows or brown sandpipers fluffing and settling on the slats underneath the dock, where they have built nests.

I swirl Dad's razor through the seawater to get all his hair stubs out. Then I snap it open, spilling the blade onto the wood. Wet and clean, it shimmers in the sun. A panic rises from deep down, and the fluttering of the birds beneath the dock seems to be inside my stomach. I hold the blade carefully between my first finger and thumb, then quickly check the white underside of flesh between my elbow and wrist. It only takes a second to run the sharpness across my arm, making a perfect line.

All that happened is flying out of me in that second — Ham falling off the bridge, his body turned, trying to grab hold of the footing, Mum reaching up to hold on to something, her face pushed into the floor, saying she doesn't want another baby, Elizabeth Ruth wiping herself with leaves in the woods between our house and Ray's.

Drops of blood appear, squeezing out the line, running a red stream toward my palm. It suddenly hurts, a real hurt I can see. Right here, pouring out of me. All the bad is finally running out of me. I'm cutting it out. I watch it trickling down my arm, knowing I'm becoming pure and clean again. I rise up toward the blue. When I spread out my arms, the whole sky is mine. It's just me and the sky facing each other. *Here I am, Ham. Look, Ham, see what I did?*

I drop Dad's metal razor and blade with a *plunk, plunk* into the water, watching them sink down into the bubbles, then disappear into the ocean. I have to wash off the blood flowing out, staining the dock an ugly brown color. When I dip my new arm in and swish it around in a tight circle, it stings so much I think I'm going to scream. I'm waiting for that Jesus-face to take over me, but the inside of my mouth is thrashing around like there's someone in there wanting to cry out, plain mad at everything.

It hurts. I scream and keep screaming out all that old dry air down there inside me. It feels so good I can't stop — not even when I notice there are red stars splattered across my yellow-flowered dress. The sky is falling, collapsing all over my dress, and I don't think I can stop screaming.

The sky is unfolding its cloudy red heavens, and I'm waiting for the Jesus-face to break through to grab hold of me and fill me with His light. I'm calling for Jesus when the sky opens like the Red Sea, paving the way inside. But it's not Jesus' face I see in there. It's my own.

9

I tuck my arm close to my side, squeezing around the middle of my forearm to keep my cut from stinging so bad. "Slap Jack," someone yells from the shed. They are all laughing, sitting around the cot, the cards in the center and the portable radio playing. When I peek through the crooked door of the shed, Luke is calling Elizabeth Ruth Jack and slapping her. Elizabeth Ruth looks stunned for a moment, then rocks forward on her feet and smacks Luke on the chin. His face goes red and his eyes flare before he breaks out laughing. I want everyone to have rules again and stop acting crazy.

"There you are. We were waiting for you. How about a swim? We're walking down to State Beach," Mum says when she sees me. "Why don't you go get your suit on?"

I see the trail of red dissolving in the seawater.

Inside the house is quiet except for the wind passing through the open windows. "Your cheatin' heart," I sing shakily, "will tell on you." I slip my feet into my shiny bathing suit and pull it up as fast as I can before Dad comes home and catches me singing with barely any clothes on. My arm brushes against my leg and starts bleeding again. I squeeze my other hand around it, watching the drops of blood push out of the skin. It hurts. The white walls flash around me.

They're not cracking, they're buzzing, and I remember when my head and my limbs ached as if I had been run over. All those people dressed in white were talking in deep voices. Where was everyone then?

My arm is throbbing now and I'm swirling in the buzz of lights.

"Emily," someone calls. "Are you ready yet, Emily?"

They are waiting for me. Sarah is reading from her Heritage dictionary, "Liver disease. Liver. Let's see, live, livelihood, lively, liver, 'a large gland in the abdomen of vertebrates that secretes bile and acts in the formation of blood and metabolism of carbohydrates, fats, proteins, minerals, and vitamins.' That's it, nothing on liver disease. Just liverwort, liverwurst —"

"Well, that's what he's going to get if he keeps drinking so much." Hope cuts her off. "He's probably at a bar right now."

"I know someone who has an uncle who had to get a liver transplant," Sarah continues.

"What if Dad has to get a whole new liver put in?" Elizabeth Ruth asks.

"They'll probably cut out yours and give it to him," Hope answers.

"Very funny," Elizabeth Ruth answers, scowling.

"No one has liver disease. Come on," Mum says, waving us on. "By the way, Elizabeth Ruth, did you take your father's razor? I saw it there before church and now it's missing. Have you been using it?"

"No."

"Are you sure?"

"Yes, I'm sure."

"Did anyone else see your father's razor anywhere?"

They all say no.

My face burns, remembering the razor go plunk into the sea. It drifts, cuts into the waves, before it disappears.

"Well, it had to go somewhere," Mum says.

"Maybe he took it with him," Hope says.

With our towels draped around our necks, we walk down to the boardwalk and along the stretch of sea. "Hmm, breathe it in." Mum stops, putting her small hand gently on her stomach and lifting her face to the sky to breathe in the ocean air. "There's nothing like it. When I was a girl, my grandfather told me to breathe in the ocean air as deep as I could, so it would go all the way to the bottom of my lungs."

We all stop to breathe the way Mum does. Way up above us, a jet is looping through the sky, propelling thick white smoke into snaky letters.

"What's it say?" Elizabeth Ruth asks.

"It says, 'Will you marry me, Elizabeth Ruth? I miss you so much. Love, your future husband, Ray,'" Hope answers, squinting into the sky.

Ray, Mr. Kosik, Willow Street, the chickens, and Cawood all seem so far away. I hope Ray has moved away by the time we get back.

"The first word is definitely *come*," Sarah says, shaping her hand into a visor over her eyes. Already, though, the word is blurring, the cloudy loops dissolving into the blue.

"'Grand,'" Elizabeth Ruth shouts as we all start down the stairs. "In the midde, it says, 'Grand.' I'm coming and I'm grand!"

"It's a grand sale, you idiot."

On the cement platform, at the bottom of the stairs, a middle-aged man and woman in dripping wet suits glance up at the sky-writing. They laugh to each other, then she takes hold of his elbow to lean over and brush the sand between her toes with the corner of a towel. As we take our sneakers off, the couple put their flip-flops on and slowly make their way up the stairs. Even though they're old, they keep laughing and talking to each other until they reach the top of the stairs and begin walking away from us, without looking back. Wait, I want to call. Something pounds inside of me, making me want to follow them wherever they are going.

I sweep my eyes across the blue sea. When I look back to the boardwalk, the couple is gone.

Owen stays sleeping in the shade of his carriage that Sarah and Hope have carried down. Mum pulls her bathing cap down over her ears, then lifts her loose dress up over her head, tossing it onto the sand.

No one notices the cut marks on my arm as we, wearing our glossy new suits, start toward the water. Elizabeth Ruth's is red and mine's too big but feels like silky air around my body as I wade into the sea with Mum.

"You won't have Nixon to kick around anymore," Luke yells, hurling himself over the waves toward John. We watch Luke sprinting from a line of seaweed on the sand into the water, doing flips, taking turns being Nixon, Superman, an Indian, or drunk like Dad. Each time he waits for John to look up at him, to laugh. I know one thing: I don't want anyone to die.

A man's bald head bobs up and down in the waves past Mum, drawing circles around herself with her small hand like a water brush. She is happy now, her eyes sparkle like the sea. Through the gray-blue-green water I can see the stones, feel their smooth shape beneath my toes. The skywriting has disappeared to nothing but white streaks melting into blue. Elizabeth Ruth is swimming around us, her arms and legs pushing out like a frog's as she surrounds us with her circles. Circles press into more circles. I see a round shape rise up out of the swirling water.

"One day I'm going to live in a round house," I tell them.

"With who?" Sarah asks.

"Whom," Mum corrects.

"Mr. Kosik?" Hope asks.

"No," I say quickly, "with all of you and Mum." I don't want to think about Mr. Kosik, or about getting married, or about any man, or even about growing tips like Hope, Sarah, and Elizabeth Ruth have showing through their bathing suits. I reach down for a handful of ocean stones and squeeze them as hard as I can to make the salt stop biting through my cut.

Hope says, "I'll live with you in your round house."

"I will, too," Sarah decides.

I pitch one of the gray stones out by Elizabeth Ruth, slipping in and out of the waves with her shaved smelt fish body. I know she will, too.

I'm sure Mum will want to live with us in the round house. She dives into the water, kicking in a one-two flutter as she reaches her gliding arms over her head, through the water, and around again, lifting her face out of the water to breathe every other stroke. No one would ever know that was a small hand like a claw carrying her body so perfectly through the ocean as she swims away.

I check the red line forming on the inside of my arm. *See, Ham, here you are.* He is here, where I broke myself open, where I let him go. I have to laugh to myself when I think of him flying from me. I thought I'd live with him forever. I spread my arms and fall into the sea, swimming through the waves, catching myself each time they wash over me.

Mum gives John twenty dollars to go to the snack stand to buy hot dogs and lemonade. She says the salt water makes us hungry and we can have two if we want. She says it's the best day she's ever seen. We sit on our towels and gulp everything. No one wants to go home.

We stay all afternoon, long after the people at the beach have brushed the sand off each other's shoulders and backs, rolled up their umbrellas and towels, packed their pails and shovels, tractors, flippers, and masks. They have squeezed the air out of their floats, loaded their arms full to carry everything back to their cars to take home to their shingled houses, where they have small yards for a clothesline, a few bikes, a dog, and rules to keep them in order — just like us, but we have no rules anymore. Not budging, we watch the sun sinking lower and lower. If we could stay right here, everything would be all right.

Sunburned and salty, we finally drape our towels back around our necks and start slowly back. The sun is hanging over the edge of the sea. No one asks what time it is or if Mum thinks he's home yet, or anything. Her hair pulled back in a ponytail and still wearing her throw-over dress, Mum decides we should walk to town to get an ice cream before we go home. She doesn't want to go back either.

I wonder when she's going to announce my party, the one she said we'd have because I'm talking again. Maybe it's a surprise.

"Get whatever you want," Mum says and waits for us to examine all the flavors. I follow her eyes, darting around the ice cream parlor, looking at the heart-shaped cushioned seats, glittering tabletops, and jukebox — everything shining back at her — until she catches a glimpse of herself in the glass behind the counter. Using her hand like a brush, she smoothes her hair out, puckers her lips as if she's putting on lipstick, and fixes her dress, straightening herself, standing taller in the mirror.

"I think Owen's hungry again, Mum," John says, passing her Owen. She pays, and we all sit at the window table eating our ice cream even though it's dinnertime. Sarah stands behind Mum, running her hands through Mum's hair, twirling and coiling it into a circle on top of her head. I lick my butter crunch cone as slowly as possible, waiting for her to tell everyone about my party. The ice cream is melting down the sides of the cone. They're all getting up. I don't think there is going to be a surprise party.

It's dark outside and the air is colder, cutting through our damp clothes. Our world is falling apart. "I'm freezing," Elizabeth Ruth whines, holding herself around the waist.

"Can't you stop complaining for once in your life?" John asks her.

"Do you think you're the only one, Elizabeth Ruth?" Hope says sharply.

"Make a bet that he's not home?" Luke asks.

When no one answers him, he asks again.

The sky fills with honking.

"They're early, the geese," Mum says. The geese are flapping loudly in the blue-black sky.

A heavy weight presses through me like a shadow falling through my body. They're telling us something, warning us as they honk gracefully through the sky like waves across the sea. We turn onto our street, and the geese fly west, leaving the dark sky behind them.

Up ahead the Oldsmobile is parked in front of our house. Mum's head jerks, pulling tight. She walks faster, clenching Owen, who starts to cry.

"What about Florida?" I say, keeping my eyes on the starless sky, looking for a sign. Mum laughs softly. My sisters lag behind and don't say anything. Hope whistles as we pass Miss Patrick's porch with the mannequin staring out to sea, her scarf sweeping around her unmoving face. I almost expect a gust of wind to carry her away.

None of our neighbors is rocking on the porch chairs watching the night sky. Through the lighted windows I see figures moving in and out of the rooms, then they are gone.

Home again, we are standing in the dark, all jumpy and bumping into each other, like we're guilty of breaking into our own house. Luke clings to Mum's dress.

"Donald?" Mum calls. "Donald, are you home?" No one answers. There is a chill in the air. Mum forgot about my party.

"Good," says Hope.

"At least he had the sense to walk," Mum mutters, sniffing the air, then pointing to an empty bottle of Jameson whisky on the kitchen table.

Mum brings her finger to her lips. "Shhh. Donald?" she calls again, cocking her head to the side as she carries Owen into the living room and sets him on the couch that swings out, creaking softly.

"He's probably at the VFW," Hope says.

"Never mind," Mum says, flicking on all the lights. "Luke, it's time for bed, wash your hands and face and brush your teeth."

"My back is killing me," Luke yells a second later from the bathroom. When John pokes Luke's back with his finger, he leaves a perfect white circle on Luke's red back.

"Stop poking me," he yells. "Why aren't *you* burned?" John lifts his shirt to show his brown skin as Mum hauls Luke into the kitchen to smear ointment all over him. Hope and Elizabeth Ruth go into the bathroom together while the rest of us watch Mum.

"Ouch, you're killing me," Luke screeches.

"Hold still," Mum says, massaging the ointment in circles across his back. I wish Mum would cover the line running across my arm with ointment, but I tuck it out of sight, holding it close to my side.

Mum opens the refrigerator to take a quick inventory and realizes there is no milk. "Your father will throw a fit if there's no milk in the morning." John has to go to the market.

After John leaves, Luke goes to his and John's bedroom and my sisters go out to the shed, the walls start caving in around me, the ceiling inches down, and everything becomes smaller.

I follow Mum while she straightens up the kitchen, then I go outside to breathe the sea air all the way to the bottom of my lungs, all the way down that black hole, then back up to my throat. A light burns inside the shed. I step closer, peeking in the window. Sitting cross-legged, Hope has Dad's wooden box on her lap. It looks so strange, its reddish wood gleaming in the sharp lights. With a huge pair of green clippers, she is cutting the padlock off Dad's box. Beside her is another padlock, still wrapped in its package. Sarah and Elizabeth Ruth stare at the box, waiting for Hope, whose mouth is a tight line across her face. Everybody is waiting to find out what Dad locked in the box.

"What if it's money?" Elizabeth Ruth asks. "Should we take it?"

"It has to be a will," Sarah says, "or a letter."

"Who would he write a letter to?" Elizabeth Ruth asks.

"Not one he wrote, one he got, stupid."

"If it's a will," Elizabeth Ruth says, "I wonder what he left us."

"What if it's the photo?" Hope asks.

"The photo?" Elizabeth Ruth repeats.

"Of Ham jumping?" Sarah asks in disbelief. "Open it."

"What's it say?" Elizabeth Ruth asks.

Everyone looks at Hope, who, for once in her life, doesn't say anything. Cold air seeps into me as I lean up against the window. I can feel the shape of me, my hips and belly, pressing against the clapboard. My breath clouds the glass. What did he do with the camera? I wonder. My sunburned skin is hot then cold, pulling tight around me. I want to be in the group.

The lock snaps and breaks off the box.

Hope takes a deep breath and removes it. She closes her eyes for a moment, then opens the box. She leans closer to the box and pushes her hand inside and pulls out a white paper. Hope's eyes are gleaming as she holds the paper in her palm.

"Unfold it," Sarah says, leaning forward. "Open it."

"I wish it was money," Elizabeth Ruth says.

Hope sits up straight and carefully opens the paper. Her eyes scan the page in disbelief.

"What's it say?" Sarah says.

"Our names. That's all it is. A list of our names." She laughs, letting the paper fly out of her hand. "Doesn't he remember who we are?"

Sarah catches it and reads, "John, Hope, Sarah, Elizabeth Ruth, Ham — but his name is crossed off — Emily, Luke, Owen."

"What's that supposed to mean?" Elizabeth Ruth asks.

"Who knows?" Hope says.

"I'm glad it's not the photo," Sarah says.

"Why? That would have been proof."

"Proof of what?"

"That Dad made Ham jump."

"You can't prove that."

"Emily could."

"Do you think she would?"

"I don't know, but I bet we could get her to."

"You really want to do that?"

Hope sets the box down. We haven't found out anything, I guess. Maybe there is nothing to know about Dad.

I back away from the window, leaving them staring at the white paper with our names listed on it. "Why'd he bother keeping it locked?" Hope asks.

Her laughter follows me back to the house, where I sneak quietly in through the kitchen door. This time, I notice one of Dad's loafers resting on its side. I hear Mum moving something in the bedroom, dragging something heavy across the floor. I walk toward her room to ask her why Dad would keep our names locked up in a box. Mum is breathing funny. The back of my neck goes cold and prickly. Mum is breathing too loud. Then it comes to me. Dad has worn these loafers every day since we got to Martha's Vineyard. He *is* home, maybe he has been here the whole time. What'd you do with the camera, Dad?

I am walking on a separate plane, above everything else in the room, tipping forward, leaning toward the partly open door to Mum's bedroom. It's like I've slid into the cold sea and whatever I've been waiting for has found me at last. It's clutching me around the throat, choking me, telling me not to say anything.

Dad is grabbing Mum's face, her waist, and thighs. His face is sweaty and swollen white and his eyes are red circles spinning at everything in his way. I hide behind the door, fitting into the crack, ready to die.

She stumbles toward him, quietly begging, "Please, Donald. The children."

"Please, Donald, the children," he mimics her in a thick voice, then laughs. "What about me? Where were you all day? What about my supper?"

"I can fix you something now." I can barely hear her. "What do you want?"

He pushes her down on the floor beside their bed, his hand on her head, smacking it softly against the floor. "You're supposed to be here when I get home. Did you think about me?" He grinds his knee into her thigh, then lets go. She moans.

I see you, Dad.

"You know what I want?" His mouth stretches into a grimace, almost a smile. "You out of my sight." He is going to either laugh or cry or break Mum's small hand, which he is twisting around until she arches her back and begins to grunt as quietly as she can.

I saw you at the bridge, Dad. What if we find the photo?

"Spoiling them again, probably. How much money did you spend today? Huh? Did you ever think about getting me supper? Huh?"

"Let me get you a drink now," she says, trying to rise from where she is sprawled.

"Don't bother." He puts all of his weight onto her, pushing himself between her legs. Mum reaches for the bedspread, which she draws over her face as Dad pushes into her, under her flowered dress. Somewhere beyond this room where Mum is being hurt is the sea pounding, howling through the depths of me. I can taste it when I suck on my arm, pressing the fleshy skin into my mouth. I suck the salt out to get rid of the fear in my mouth.

"Donald, please, stop. I don't want —" Mum cries through the cloth.

He pushes her face to the side.

The wind blows through the room. I take my hand from my mouth. This time, I tell myself, I have to do something. I step out of the crack, into the living room. I'm going to walk out the kitchen door to find my sisters.

I know what happened the last time when Dad saw me watching him hurt Mum. When I ran toward the kitchen door, something smashed into me — a brick or a bottle hit the back of my head and fell through me. My knees buckled underneath me, I fell through the glass, and I landed right here on the walkway. I was running away from Dad, then everything went black.

When I woke I was spinning around a room with white walls. The first thing I did was throw up all over the front of my white johnny, down the sides of the sheets, spraying the metal wheels of the bed and the tiles that were speckled pebbles. People clomped through the hallway outside and a buzzing noise clamped onto the inside of my ear. The smells of the floor polish and throw up stung my nose. When I looked at the light on the white ceiling, I knew Ham was there, but I never saw him. He was dead.

Someone was watching *The Price Is Right* behind a green curtain that divided the room in two. I could see the TV propped on a metal arm bent at the elbow, but I couldn't see anyone. On the tray beside my bed was a mound of dark meat hardened in a thick gravy next to stringy wax beans. The front of my johnny was streaked with brown clumps.

Dad was the first one to visit me. As soon as he came into the room, I knew it was my fault Ham drowned. "Hi, kiddo," Dad said, standing at the edge of my bed, fingering the loose sheets.

My mouth opened.

"No, no, no," he said. He put up his hand to stop me. His eyes shifted.

"Shhh," he murmured. "You've been in shock."

Through the stink of my throw up, I could smell the alcohol on his breath.

"Nothing, nothing, nothing," he said, backing up. He pressed the silver button. "Everything will be all right now."

It wasn't though. I couldn't talk. I couldn't say anything to anyone. I could never tell them what happened. Nothing was all right and Mum wasn't there.

I see Ham with his blue skin and red mouth and I know he never talked to me in the car on the way to the hospital because he couldn't. They took him away from me. But he is still mine. He is inside me. It wasn't my fault or Dad's fault.

I hold my head between my hands to stop everything, telling myself I *can* talk now. Ham isn't here, but Mum is and my sisters are.

I have to help Mum. Nothing can happen to Mum. When I am close enough to hear the music from Hope's radio, I call out to my sisters. "Hurry," I tell them. "Help me, he's hurting her."

They follow me inside to the bedroom door which is now closed. Elizabeth Ruth is already crying, she's so scared. But we're all in this together. "Open it," I whisper.

They're on the floor next to the bed, Dad straddled over Mum, his hand smothering her mouth. Her dress pushed up, Mum's chest is moving up and down too fast. She tilts her face toward us. Beads of his sweat drop onto her face. He doesn't notice us yet. "Who's in charge around here?" he asks loudly. She cannot answer him.

"Leave her alone," Hope yells. His head snaps back, his eyes dragging slowly over all of us. He half-laughs at us, stretching his lips into a tight smile, cracking his face. Then, in the next second, Dad's face breaks, his shoulders give in, and all of him collapses into a heap on top of Mum.

Where are you, Mum?

Hope grabs him under the arms and tries to pull him off of Mum. He rolls against the wall, bringing his knees close to his chest. Mum covers her face with her hands. "I'm sorry you had to see this," she says as she lifts herself up.

"How long has he been doing this to you, Mum?" Hope asks, out of breath. "Why didn't you tell us?"

"It's all right," my mother answers.

"No, it's not all right. It's not all right. It's not, it's not, it's not all right," Hope yells over Dad.

Sarah and I sit on the end of the bed, on either side of Mum, who finally uncovers her blotchy red face. Here is Mum, who is supposed to keep me safe, crying like a baby, and there is Dad, who says he is the strongest man alive, curled up against the wall. Elizabeth Ruth runs to get a roll of toilet paper for Mum to wipe her nose. Luke stands with an open mouth outside the doorway.

"I thought things were going to change," Hope says. "Things *are* going to change."

We all stand there, waiting for things to become normal again, waiting for everything to be how it was before.

Then Dad, with his belt unbuckled, his pants hanging off of him, and his puffy face smudged with grime, does something we've never seen him do before. He starts crying. I didn't think Dad could cry. I watch carefully to make sure when he turns his head it's really him.

"Sorry. I'm sorry." I don't think he's fooling us.

Footsteps cross the kitchen.

"Dad? Is that Dad?" John's eyes circle us slowly, taking everything in. His shoulders straighten and he stands taller. "What happened?"

Dad is a mess. He spills himself out in front of us. His face to the wall, he rocks back and forth on the floor. "I'm sorry," he sobs. "I'm sorry, John."

I want to believe him.

Luke comes closer, trying to figure out what's happening. I make room for him on the bed. Mum's face has changed. She's smiling, her face all lit up again, her arms wrapped around Luke. "Hope's right. Things are going to change around here," Mum finally says. "The past is past."

I go to him, kneel down, and lay my arm across his back. He is cold and shivering. I am so near I can see the inside of his ear like the hollow of a shell. "Dad," I say, "are you there?"

He rolls unsteadily toward me, then holds me with his eyes like melting pools.

"I-I-I," he begins. "Ham —" Then he throws his head back. We all turn toward Mum sitting on the edge of the bed, pulled away from the wall and stripped of sheets and blankets.

Owen starts to cry from the other room. She walks to get him. I feel my breath moving through me. Mum says you can't always change people, but you can change yourself. I roll my tongue in my mouth. "Say you won't hurt her again," I say.

"I won't hurt anybody," he whispers. "I never wanted anything to happen to Ham. I'd do anything to have him here again." He throws his head back once more, his eyes rolling up to the ceiling as if they could escape his face. "I'm going to be good from now on, I promise."

Bud trots into the room, cocks his head, and licks Dad's wet face. We can't help but laugh. With Owen in her arms, Mum comes to Dad's side. "It's all over now. Come on, let's get up." She touches his hand.

Suddenly I think he might forget everything he's promised by tomorrow and it will all be the same. What if he never changes at all? I'm still changed. As Dad leans forward, rising, the whole room shifts. I catch my breath. What I want to say to him is, Wait, Dad, tell me about Ham. Say something else. Confess. But already it's like I'm swimming, pushing right through the clear blue, past the feathery seaweed, the pink-gray stones, black mussels, and broken pieces of clamshells, and all of it pushing right through me. It's all so sharp and clear, as if I've never really been swimming underwater before.

I lift my face to listen for the sound of the birds and hear nothing, not a flutter, not a sign of the bluebird. Ham isn't here now. Just the watery blue of Dad's eyes. When my eyes meet his, I begin to see everything that has passed.